D J Dodds
March 1994

Creeping Jenny

Creeping Jenny

John Sherwood

Charles Scribner's Sons
New York

Maxwell Macmillan Canada
Toronto

Maxwell Macmillan International
New York   Oxford   Singapore   Sydney

Copyright © 1993 by John Sherwood

First United States Edition

Charles Scribner's Sons   Maxwell Macmillan Canada, Inc.
Macmillan Publishing Company   1200 Eglinton Avenue East
866 Third Avenue   Suite 200
New York, NY 10022   Don Mills, Ontario M3C 3N1

Macmillan Publishing Company is part of the Maxwell Communication
Group of Companies.

Library of Congress Cataloging-in-Publication Data
Sherwood, John, 1913–
    Creeping Jenny/John Sherwood.—1st U.S. ed.
    p.   cm.
    ISBN 0-684-19613-1
    1. Grant, Celia (Fictitious character)—Fiction.   2. Women detectives—
England—Fiction.   3. Women gardeners—England—Fiction.
I. Title.
PR6037.H517C7   1993   93–26576   CIP
823'.914—dc20

Macmillan books are available at special discounts for bulk purchases for
sales promotions, premiums, fund-raising, or educational use. For details,
contact: Special Sales Director, Macmillan Publishing Company,
866 Third Avenue, New York, NY 10022

10 9 8 7 6 5 4 3 2

Printed in the United States of America

Acknowledgements

The passage quoted on pp. 109–10 is reproduced by kind permission of Dr M. Ladle of the Institute of Freshwater Ecology at Wareham, to whom the author is also indebted for valuable advice.

Prologue

It was a day of ill omen at Archerscroft Nurseries, with everything possible going wrong. During the night a branch blown from a tree by the high wind had broken two panes in the alpine house. As it was raining heavily, the rock plants underneath the hole had been drenched, a state of affairs which no self-respecting alpine will tolerate. Half the staff were away with colds or flu, and all sorts of routine jobs were in arrears. A batch of the scented *Cyclamen libanoticum* was showing signs of cyclamen mite, and just before closing time one of the girls had tripped over something and upset a tray of *Haemanthus coccineus* offsets into a puddle, throwing most of them out of their pots.

Having coped with all this and refreshed herself with a much-needed bath and a whisky, Celia Grant gulped down a sandwich and left her cosy fireside reluctantly to attend a meeting. She would have been even more reluctant if she could have foreseen the ominous consequences that the business transacted would provoke. It would be absurd to compare a decision taken at a meeting of the Melbury Garden Society with the quarrel between Agamemnon and Achilles about a concubine, which launched Homer into his epic tragedy about the Trojan War. Nevertheless, events at that Garden Society meeting were to bring in their train long-term consequences which reached far beyond the village of Melbury.

Fortunately the meetings were held within easy walking distance, at the home of Admiral Bond, the society's leading light. The Admiral's age was a much discussed

1

secret, but informed sources claimed that he was at least eighty. The death of his sensible wife a few years back had left him adrift in a sea of his own humours and eccentricities, and in control of her considerable fortune. He had arrogated to himself the office of president of the society on the death of the previous incumbent without giving up his existing post as secretary, and tended to treat the rest of the members as the crew of his flagship, subject to naval discipline and exposed to dire penalties if they mutinied.

Celia had been co-opted very unwillingly on to the committee because of events not of her making. She had decided that this time Archerscroft Nurseries would not have a stand at the Chelsea Flower Show in the following May. Exhibiting there was all very well for the big operators who mounted massive displays of eye-catching floral overkill. Smaller firms with modest stands tended to get overlooked in the crowded tent. She would do her duty on the judges' day as a judge on Floral Committee B, then leave quietly for home before the crowds arrived.

But this sensible plan had been frustrated by the Admiral. As President of the Garden Society he had been notified by Chelsea's organizers, the Royal Horticultural Society, of a competition for local organizations affiliated to it to enter. They were to submit designs for patio-sized courtyard gardens. Organizations submitting the eight best entries would be invited to construct and plant their garden in one of the eight small brick enclosures constructed for the purpose in an opening off the main avenue of the show.

Without consulting anyone the Admiral had decided that they would compete and had sent for application forms. The membership's alarm at this was softened when he revealed that he would meet the quite considerable expense of constructing and planting the garden if, as he confidently expected, the society's entry was among the eight best. Realizing, however, that even a buttonhole organized by him would be an administrative disaster, they had begged Celia to come to the rescue and produce a design which could be submitted for approval to the RHS.

This she had done, in the teeth of constant interference by the Admiral. His own garden was a riot of well-heads and pergolas and little Japanese bridges and naked cherubs blowing penny whistles. He had tried to bully Celia into incorporating as many of these ornaments as possible in a design for a courtyard garden measuring thirteen feet by ten. Supported by the membership, she had beaten him down to one naked cherub, and submitted a neat, uncluttered design. It was too late now to make any but the most minor alterations, but the Admiral had not grasped this. She would certainly have to defend her design at the meeting against a determined guerrilla attack from him.

As she picked her way up the front path of his over-prettified Elizabethan farmhouse she wondered who would be at the meeting. Since joining the committee she had become the informal leader of the opposition, but a sparse attendance on a wet December night might well leave her in a minority of one.

Glancing round the Admiral's oak refectory table, she saw only one reliable supporter. James Carstairs, a lecturer at the local polytechnic with a divorce pending, had made civilized overtures to her, which she had rejected with equal civility. It was not clear whether he classed himself as an admirer who still lived in hopes or simply as a friend, but as he always voted with her it hardly mattered. Wilfrid Edgeley, who sat next to James, knew nothing about gardening and only attended the meetings to get away from a wife who bullied him mercilessly. Having an independent income and a total vacuum between the ears, he had never pursued any gainful occupation. He was very handsome in a vapid blond way, but very nervous. He always voted with the Admiral because the Admiral shouted at him if he did otherwise.

Further down the table was Fred Tunney, who grew huge mop-headed dahlias in rows in his vegetable garden, and won prizes for them at local shows. As a leading member of the council-house mafia, he resented the

3

dominance of the gentry in village affairs. During the great village crisis* three years ago Celia had been responsible for exposing Fred's cousin George as a murderer and a child abuser, and the Tunney family had not forgiven her. He therefore tended to resist the Admiral's more outrageous proposals unless they were also resisted by Celia, whom he hated.

The other six members were willingly or reluctantly carried along on the Admiral's bandwagon, though one of them, the Hon. Mrs Cadogan, was a personal friend who often managed to knock sense into him in private while supporting him in public.

He called the meeting to order and announced the first item on the agenda. 'Minutes of the last meeting.'

Having bought and mastered a word processor, he had put it to intensive use. The result was an avalanche of agendas, discussion papers, and minutes of meetings, the last-named often reflecting his own views rather than what the committee had decided. The minutes of the previous meeting, of which everyone had been sent a copy, were no exception.

With his pen poised, he glanced round the table. 'No objections? Then I'll sign the minutes.'

'Steady on, George,' said Celia. 'Last time we had before us an application for membership of the society from Mrs Fortescue of Kenlake Manor. We agreed after discussion to defer a decision till this meeting.'

The 'discussion' at the previous meeting had consisted of an indefensible attempt by the Admiral to turn down Mrs Fortescue's application because he had quarrelled with her husband, a reason which made even his own groupies stir in their chairs uneasily.

'It ought to have been in the minutes,' Celia persisted, 'and we ought to deal with it now under matters arising.'

Admiral Bond looked put out. 'Well, you all know what I think about this.'

They did. Jason Fortescue, the applicant's husband, was an international financier who spent most of his time

* See *A Bouquet of Thorns* (Macmillan, 1989)

4

jet-setting round the world and supervising the affairs of Hanbury-Fortescue Holdings, a huge conglomerate with ramifications in every continent. On the rare occasions when he came to rest at Kenlake Manor he upset the Admiral by seeming to set up a rival claim to be the squire and patron of the village. The two had soon fallen out over an appeal for funds to repair the village hall. Fortescue had accused the Admiral, from a position of superior financial expertise, of making a muddle, and they were not on speaking terms.

'The feller's a crook,' the Admiral thundered. 'He whizzes round the world making takeover bids with money he hasn't got, and fiddling the books to deceive his accountants and stuffing money away in private banks in the Seychelles, and borrowing huge sums in a desperate attempt to stop the whole thing collapsing. Not to speak of dishing out lawsuits right left and centre.'

This was a favourite theme of the Admiral's. Apart from one lawsuit which had made notorious headlines, no one knew of any foundation for his allegations.

'You have no evidence for saying that,' said James Carstairs angrily.

'Well it stands to reason, doesn't it? He's not even British, he's an immigrant from Central Europe who changed his name from something unpronounceable when he got here. They all overreach themselves and come to grief in the end.'

This too was a fantasy of the Admiral's imagination. It occurred to Celia that he might well come to grief himself in an action for slander, but she decided not to raise the temperature by saying so. The courtyard garden competition was the next item on the agenda. The chances of a successful outcome were slim if the meeting degenerated into a brawl.

'Anyway,' he went on, 'we don't want the Fortescues pushing their way in here and telling us how to run our affairs.'

'My wife knows Mrs Fortescue quite well,' said Wilfrid Edgeley timidly. 'She seems very pleasant.'

'Only a mental defective would have married a man

5

like that,' thundered the Admiral, whereupon Wilfrid subsided.

'She's a very nice woman and a customer of mine,' said Celia, who had laid out the garden at Kenlake Manor shortly after the Fortescues moved in.

'Well,' said the Admiral, 'shall we go on to the next business?'

Celia decided that brawl or no brawl, she could not let this pass. But before she could speak, James Carstairs took her place in the firing line. 'No!' he protested. 'Not till we've decided about Mrs Fortescue's application.'

From across the table Mrs Cadogan was signalling unobtrusively to Celia. Cool it, the message read, don't start a row. I know he's being impossible, but he'll see reason if I talk to him quietly afterwards.

'Strictly speaking,' said the Admiral, 'this isn't a matter for the committee. The admission of new members is dealt with by the secretary.'

Down at the far end Fred Tunney banged the table with his fist. 'Some people are getting too big for their boots,' he remarked in his slow, earthy vegetable garden voice. 'The secitary jest takes the money and gives the new members a receipt, it's not his business to pick and choose.'

'Quite right,' said Carstairs firmly. 'It's for the committee to decide.'

'The decision's taken already,' said the Admiral. 'After we discussed this last month I acted on what I took to be the sense of the meeting and wrote to Mrs Fortescue refusing her application.'

'In that case,' said Wilfrid Edgeley, deflated, 'there's nothing to be done.'

'What grounds did you give for refusing?' asked one of the Admiral's groupies uneasily.

'I said we were very sorry, but we couldn't accept applications from people who lived outside the parish boundary.'

There was a stunned silence. Celia could contain herself no longer. 'But look here, George, she's only just outside. And there are four people sitting round this table who live further away than she does.'

6

'Yes, George,' said Mrs Cadogan. 'You'd better watch out, there'll be trouble about this.'

'There will, surely,' boomed Fred Tunney. 'Mr Fortescue, he paid up handsome over the village hall repairs. He's been a good friend to the village.'

'There are others living here who contribute as much as he does,' said the Admiral testily. 'Some of them might think there was no need for them to dip into their pockets if we're all going to rely on Mr Fortescue.'

This was a coded threat. Having been left a massive fortune by his late wife, he reckoned to head the list of contributors to local good causes. Not for the first time, he was hinting that the cash flow would dry up if he was thwarted.

'So shall we pass on now to the next business?' he said firmly.

Celia's all-important item was next on the agenda. She knew she would be outvoted and decided not to object. Nor, with money on their minds, did any of the others. They were not to know that in their humdrum way they were taking part in the opening scene of a Greek-style tragedy, in which overweening arrogance is punished by vengeful gods.

'You mark my words,' boomed Fred Tunney, 'upsettin' Mr Fortescue will surely lead to trouble.'

The Admiral ignored him. 'Next business. Preparations for Chelsea.'

This was Celia's cue. Before the meeting she had given everyone copies of the design she had submitted, incorporating amendments agreed at the previous meeting. The Admiral studied it in discontented silence. 'It looks a bit bleak, doesn't it. I still think the cherub will look insignificant in the middle of the pool, we need something bigger. How about my lead stork?'

'It's huge,' Celia objected. 'Why not Nelson's Column from Trafalgar Square?' She looked round at the others for support and elicited embarrassed murmurs of agreement, in which even his groupies joined.

'Then let's have the little bronze cannon off my front lawn. Yes, I think that would be best.'

7

'A garden is supposed to be a peaceful place,' protested James Carstairs. 'Why put a cannon in it?'

The Admiral snorted. 'Oh, well, if you're a pacifist.'

'The cannon's too long,' Celia objected. 'It would more or less fill the pool.'

'Then put it on a plinth in the bed just behind there,' said the Admiral brightly.

'George, I've sent the design in.'

'Can't you send them a revised version?'

There was an embarrassed silence, till Fred Tunney rumbled into speech. 'I reckon we oughter stick to what we decided in the first place.'

The silence which followed was broken by a discontented grunt from the Admiral, which Celia decided not to interpret as disagreement. 'Then shall we consider the matter settled?'

'Oh, do what you like, don't mind me,' he muttered.

On this ominously unsettled note the meeting presently ended.

Wilfrid Edgeley returned home to find his wife, the headmistress of the local comprehensive school, deep in a government white paper on education policy. 'I'm back,' he announced.

'So I see.'

'You'll never guess what the Admiral's done. Turned down Margaret Fortescue's application for membership without consulting anyone.'

'Well, what did you expect? He's half mad. I don't understand why you decided to take up with all those second-rate Garden Society people.'

'Don't be such a shrew, Grace. You kept telling me to get out from under your feet and take up something.'

'Yes. Local History or geology or Save the Children, something sensible like that.'

'They aren't all second-rate. Mrs Grant isn't.'

'Anyone can have a figure like a schoolgirl and a good complexion and pretty white hair, and still be second-rate. And there's no point in your hanging round her like a randy he-goat, you won't get anywhere. She's got a toy-boy, had him for years. That blond young man who's supposed to be her head gardener. Disgusting, he's half her age.'

'Bill Wilkins? Oh, come, Grace, that's nonsense.'

'No. You ask anyone in the village.'

'They dislike her because of what happened over Wilkins being accused of murder. When she got him off and found the real murderer she unearthed a horrible scandal affecting a whole generation of men in the village.'

'That's what she says she did. The truth's quite different. She was determined to get her toy-boy off, so she went around the place making an idiotic fuss while the police worked away quietly till they found the real culprit. I'm told she fancies herself as a sort of detective, but being nosy doesn't mean you aren't bone stupid.'

'She knows a lot about plants, and that nursery of hers is a roaring success.'

'Anyone can be a competent shopkeeper if they give their mind to it, Wilfrid. I believe she has some sort of degree from a horticultural college, but what does that amount to as an intellectual discipline? Nothing.'

So saying, she went back to her government White Paper. Her own degree was in philosophy and mathematics. She was thus unfamiliar with the wise observation of an ancient Greek playwright, to the effect that those whom the gods would destroy, they first drive mad.

One

What's got into me, thought Celia Grant crossly. There's nothing wrong with her, why don't I like her?

The girl had dressed carefully for the interview, in slacks and sensible shoes to indicate a down-to-earth attitude to work, and a Hermes scarf to add a hint of well-heeled sophistication. But slacks struck the wrong note for her, too modern. She would have been more at home in a medieval robe clutching a harp, posing for one of the Pre-Raphaelite painters. Her skin was pale and transparent, and paper-thin on the lids of watery blue eyes. Neck-length blonde hair hanging in wispy curls framed a long face with delicately moulded features. She's beautiful, Celia thought, but in a sickly way that gives me the creeps.

She picked up the girl's neatly typed CV from her desk. Jennifer Watson. Education: St Elizabeth's, Bath, a girl's boarding school with a first-class reputation. Good A-levels, including one in botany. Hoping for a place at an agricultural college in the autumn to take a degree course in horticulture.

'Which colleges have you applied to?' Celia asked.

The poor child was agonizingly shy. Her lips opened, but very little sound came out. 'Wye. And Cannington as my second choice.' After a longish pause she added: 'Most people call me Jenny.'

I must be kind to this girl, Celia thought. More years ago than she cared to remember, she too had faced exactly the same situation in the same state of inner turmoil. Panic-stricken with shyness, she had had to leave

10

home to study horticulture at prestigious Wye College, a branch of London University nestling under the chalk downs of Kent. In due course she had emerged with a Master's degree and an engagement ring. A happy marriage and two grown-up children later, she had found herself a widow with too little to do. Archerscroft Nurseries, started as a hobby, had proved a roaring commercial success. She was tiny and young-looking for her age, but from the point of view of the eighteen-year-old facing her across the desk, her prematurely white hair probably labelled her as a formidable old lady.

'Tell me a bit about yourself, Jenny. What decided you to take up horticulture?'

'My mother . . . had a lovely garden. I used to help her and . . . I got interested.'

Why the past tense? Was the mother dead? How could one phrase the question tactfully?

'You don't help her any more?'

A flicker of distress crossed Jenny's pale face. 'She married again and went to live in Canada.'

Perhaps there had been a messy divorce. To lose the support of a mother was a disaster for a shy, insecure teenage girl. I was right, Celia thought, to suspect that something's very wrong, but it's not her fault. She can't help her creepy death's-head prettiness, and I mustn't let myself be put off by it.

'So what you're looking for, Jenny,' she said, 'is a temporary job to see you through the spring and summer till you go to college. Why did you choose Archerscroft to apply to?'

Jenny hesitated. 'I tried here first because I thought . . . a smallish nursery dealing with unusual plants would be better experience.'

She was sitting very still with a resigned droop to her shoulders, as if she had already decided that there was no hope of being taken on. But there is a vacancy, Celia thought, and I ought to put her into it. Paula Berridge, one of her helpers from the village, would be going on leave in a week's time to have her first baby, and for the present there was no qualified replacement in sight. Though they would be very short-handed without Paula during the busy spring season, they could manage. But here was a temporary replacement being offered up on a plate, with only a beginner's wages to pay and no hassle when Paula wanted her job back in the autumn.

But even under supervision an ignorant teenager could do enormous damage among the Archerscroft rarities. Paula had worked at the nursery for four years, and knew what she was doing. Admittedly Jenny had helped her mother, but only in a private garden, and what did that amount to? How much, if anything, did she know?

There was only one way to find out. 'Let's have a look round the place, shall we?'

With a meek smile of thanks Jenny rose to follow her. She moved with a slow, flowing grace which went with the unearthly appearance. Creepy was the right word, that amount of languor belonged in the nineteenth century, along with anaemia and dying of consumption in one's teens.

Murmurs from Jenny as they toured the frame yard and glasshouses established that she knew the difference between a zonal and a regal pelargonium, and could identify a half-grown ligularia from its black stems, but she was baffled when confronted with the rarer items which were the backbone of Archerscroft's stock in trade. As was to be expected, *Hibiscus rosa-sinensis, Chimaphila maculata*, and *Ptelea trifoliata* meant nothing to her.

Celia took her into the potting shed and put a tray of seedlings in front of her. 'D'you know what these are?'

'Some sort of . . . pansies or violas?' She looked at the label, which bore only a set of figures, and added in her throaty near-whisper: 'A new variety? Something you've hybridized?'

She was right. The seedlings were the result of an unsuccessful cross between various perennial violas, in which the worst features of all the parents and grandparents had been reproduced.

'Shouldn't they be pricked out?' Jenny murmured.

'Yes. Let's see you do it.'

Celia foresaw what would happen. Like most amateurs she would make a mess of it. But that hardly mattered. These misbegotten seedlings were expendable.

Jenny drew a tray towards her and filled it slowly with compost from the bin below the bench. 'Is this a peat-based compost?'

It was said on a faintly peevish note and sounded like a complaint. Celia felt put on the defensive. 'Yes. For this sort of thing there's no real substitute for peat, but we use coir or mulches when we can. Are you very green and environmental?'

'I don't know much about it.' A longish pause followed. 'But I do worry, yes.'

'I worry too. We get our peat from a firm that's very conscientious about keeping up the water table. We use predatory insects to control whitefly and red spider in the glasshouses, and we only use eco-friendly chemicals.'

Jenny picked up a seedling trowel and gave it a drugged look, as if wondering what to do with it. Then she set to work. To Celia's surprise there was nothing tentative about her approach to the job. She was pricking out the seedlings methodically, starting at one end of the tray and lifting them one by one with the practised, economical movements which normally went with experience in a commercial nursery. Was she really a beginner straight from school? Looking at her, Celia suddenly saw a young woman ten years older. But she dismissed the sight as a hallucination.

'Well done,' she commented. 'Most amateurs dig into the box anyhow and leave half the seedlings lying on the surface, once they've got as many pricked out as they want.'

'We never did that,' said Jenny. 'We used to raise the lot, and Mum gave away what we didn't need to friends and sales for charity.'

Bill Wilkins came into the potting shed carrying a tray of rooted regal pelargonium cuttings, and looked surprised when he saw a stranger.

13

'This is Jenny,' said Celia. 'She has a place at Wye in the autumn, and wants a summer job.'

'Hi, Jenny,' said Bill.

'Bill is our head gardener,' Celia explained.

'Hi,' Jenny whispered, and went on working away at her box of seedlings without looking up. Celia suspected that her shyness became paralytic in the presence of men.

Bill was watching Jenny's busy hands and taking very little notice of the rest of her. Like her, he was avoiding eye contact. Celia looked on with amusement. He was what the women's magazines called a gorgeous blonde hunk, with very blue eyes and muscles bulging beneath his T-shirt, so that the sight of him tended to provoke hysteria in young girls and ecstasies of predatory lust in otherwise sensible housewives. Ever since Celia had known him, he had been puritanical about sex, and became rigid with indignation at the first signs of unrequited female passion. Anthea Clarkson, the only serious girlfriend in his life, had died under shocking circumstances, and since then he had lived, as far as anyone knew, in a state of monk-like chastity.

Having satisfied himself that Jenny knew what she was doing, he turned his attention to the tray of regal pelargoniums he had brought in. 'What's all this then, Celia? I just found them, they been overlooked.'

Celia considered them. They were a new departure, an interesting colour break in one of the improved varieties which could be relied on to bush out and stay in flower all summer instead of producing a flush in June followed by a permanent fit of the sulks. But they were still in the 2½-inch pots that they had been planted in as rooted cuttings.

'Horrors,' said Celia. 'Why weren't they dealt with with the rest of the batch?'

'They was down the far end, behind them hostas. Who put them there? That's what I'd like to know.'

Celia picked up one of them. 'Jenny, what d'you make of that?'

The girl took it from her in her long pale fingers. Roots

14

were growing through the bottom of the pot. 'Doesn't it need potting on?'

'You can say that again, it should have been done weeks ago. What size of pot would you use?'

'A five-inch.'

'Not a four and a half?'

'No. We used to grow them at home. They get too big for a four and a half.'

'Would you feed it?'

'Not yet. Liquid potash when the buds begin to show colour.'

'Is that what your mother did? She must have been quite an expert gardener.'

The girl's pale blue eyes met hers, but not comfortably. 'She was.'

Celia beckoned Bill outside for a consultation. To hire anyone without his OK would be courting trouble.

'She could fill in while Paula's away. What d'you think?'

'I dunno. She's so quiet, is she mental or something?'

'Just shy, I think. She seems to know quite a lot. If you keep an eye on her, she could be useful.'

'OK then, if you think so.'

Jenny had gone on pricking out the misbegotten violas. Celia took the plunge. 'I think we can find room for you till the autumn.'

'Oh. Thank you.' That was all, apart from a faint smile of pleasure which might or might not be a cover for a stronger reaction.

'Let's go back to the office, shall we, and fix it up.'

In the outer office, she settled Jenny down to have her personal details entered on the computer. This was a recent innovation, as also was Monica Porter, the red-haired young woman who presided over it and caused everything, from the weekly wage bill to the parentage of hybridized hellebores, to disappear into it out of Celia's reach. Monica was manically possessive about her machine and behaved like a demented guard dog if anyone else approached it. Celia, who had intended to

15

master it herself, found herself frustrated. And she had been further discouraged from wrestling with it by the teething troubles of her doctor, who had recently acquired a computer system. Urged by her to record the fact that she was allergic to penicillin, he had inadvertently conjured up on the screen a list of all the ills that could afflict the penis, including unexpected ones like curvature. His desperate attempts to banish this embarrassing display had failed and it had remained there throughout the consultation.

Faced with such a discouraging precedent, Celia found it difficult to resist Monica's warning that there would be chaos and ruin if anyone else touched her precious plaything. But she could not bring herself to like Monica, who lived aggressively up to her self-image as the perfect secretary. Her desk was always offensively tidy, and she made sudden attacks on the comfortable disorder of Celia's, so that papers she was working on had to be retrieved from a filing system which only Monica understood. Her neat blouses and skirts were a constant, perhaps deliberate, reproach to Celia's casual working clothes.

'And your address, Jennifer?' she was saying with her hands poised over the computer console.

'I haven't got one. I've left school and my mother's gone to Canada.'

Overhearing this through the open door of the inner office, Celia was surprised. She had assumed for some reason that Jenny lived locally.

'Then you'll be wanting lodgings in the village, won't you?' she said, standing in the doorway. 'Monica, what about old Mrs Parsons? She's been wanting a student or someone to live in, why don't you give her a ring?'

Waiting for the call to come through, Jenny sat slumped in her chair, like a passenger whose train was not due for several hours. Meanwhile fat, jolly Mary Basset from the packing shed came in from the frame yard with a list of plants for postal dispatch. Having given Jenny the once-over she shut the door of the inner office behind her and lowered her voice mischievously. 'It's alive! I thought at first it was a waxwork.'

'I know, I've been strongly tempted to stick a pin in her and see if anything happens. We're hiring her to fill in while Paula's away.'

'Ooh, Celia. Is that wise?'

'Probably not, she gives me the creeps, but I was sorry for her.' She was already having second thoughts. Why on earth had she been foolish enough to hire a girl who was obviously suffering from a mass of frantic hang-ups?

On the way out Mary stopped for a moment. 'By the way Celia dear, you need to watch that *Lysimachia nummularia*. It looks very sick to me, mind it doesn't die on you.'

Celia peered through the open door at Jenny in the outer office. If she had recognized the botanical name for Creeping Jenny, she gave no sign of it.

In the middle of February Celia was surprised and not wholly pleased to learn that her design for the courtyard garden had found favour with the RHS. The garden would actually have to be constructed and planted at Chelsea. The next step was to send in more detailed drawings of the layout and a planting plan, listing all the shrubs and herbaceous material she intended to use. She prepared all this and took it to a specially summoned meeting of the Garden Society.

'Celia, why do we have to do this now?' Admiral Bond complained. 'There's masses of time before Chelsea, can't we make up our minds later?'

'No, George. They have to know so that they get the right garden into the right courtyard. They don't want to put our old-world pink and white scheme next to a violent purple and orange job that would clash with it horribly.'

He studied the drawings discontentedly. 'I still think it looks very bare and poverty-stricken. Can't we put my stork up at the back somewhere, between the arbour and the little maple?'

Celia pointed out that the RHS would not accept major

changes in the design at this stage. Nevertheless, he returned to the charge with an attempt to reintroduce his bronze cannon. Supported by the membership, she beat off this attack.

'But they'll let us make minor changes, you say. Those white roses you've got trained up the arbour, now. They won't have much impact, will they? How about something more colourful like Climbing Masquerade?'

She opposed this on practical grounds. Roses wanted for Chelsea had to be reserved months in advance from specialist firms which forced them into bloom early in containers. She had already ordered six white Swan Lakes, and it was too late to change the order.

Coming to her support, James Carstairs asked what colour Masquerade was.

'It's a scarlet and yellow bicolour,' Celia told him, trying not to sound disgusted by it.

'I thought so, a hideous thing that would clash with everything for miles around. Why can't we leave Celia's design alone?'

Faced with united opposition from the rest of the meeting, the Admiral gave way ungraciously and she considered the matter settled. But when the minutes landed on her desk two days later, her eyes lighted on the following:

> The design for the courtyard garden at Chelsea was considered, and approved with minor amendments. It was decided that the lead stork from the President's garden should be located at the back of the exhibit to give height, and that his bronze cannon should be placed on a plinth immediately behind the pool. The cherub originally intended to be positioned in the pool to be omitted.

Celia rang the Admiral in a fury. 'How dare you, George? What's all this nonsense?'

'Nonsense, Celia? I fail to catch your meaning.'

'In the minutes, cluttering the place up with storks and guns.'

'Oh, that. I decided suddenly that the whole thing was going to look a bit bare and needed jazzing up. We ought to have a rethink.'

'But look here, the minutes of a meeting are supposed to be a record of what's been decided. You can't treat them as a scribbling pad on which to jot down whatever sudden fancies happen to pass through your head.'

'Oh, I don't know. There's no harm in flying an occasional kite.'

'You can't fly kites at Chelsea.'

'Oh come, aren't you being a bit stuffy about this?'

'No. You have to stick to the rules.' Giving him up as a hopeless case, she rang Mrs Cadogan, who promised to talk sense into him.

As winter gave way to spring the weeks passed busily. On top of the normal routine of the nursery, the supplies needed for Chelsea had to be organized, and she had too much to do to worry much about a junior employee's tormented psyche. Jenny Watson's appearance and manner still gave her the creeps, but she found no reason to repent of hiring her. Kept on routine jobs by Bill, she carried them out reliably and gave no trouble. Though still morbidly shy, she managed to take a certain amount of gentle ribbing from the women workers, but seemed terrified of men.

There was more to her, however, than shy young girl-hood. More than once Celia caught her stealing admiring glances at Bill in his muscular blond glory. On one occasion when he was busy in one of the glasshouses with a batch of *Aster frikartii*, Celia came in and saw Jenny standing motionless at the far end of the house, gazing at him. To call her look admiring was an understatement. Her mouth had dropped open in a display of unbridled sexual greed. Under her demure exterior the silly girl was obviously a boiling sexpot and a pushover for handsome men.

When she saw she was observed, she gave a start and went on loading Paulownias on to a trolley and taking them outside to harden off.

19

'Goodness me, did you see that?' murmured Mary Basset, who was standing beside Celia.

'Yes. It must be the spring weather. For a moment she looked quite ill with lust.'

Mary suppressed a giggle. 'Like a cow that wants the bull. If his nibs catches her gaping at him like that, he'll half kill her.'

Celia nodded. Bill behaved brutally to lovesick maidens on the staff, hounding and bullying them until they resigned in floods of tears.

'You'd never have thought it of her, would you?' Mary went on. 'But they say still waters run deep, don't they?'

'I don't think the waters are still, Mary. Just under rigid control. Underneath it's probably more like what goes on inside a washing machine.'

Thinking over this episode later, Celia wondered. Jenny seemed to be a mixed-up kid, but could anyone really be so shy and at the same time so greedy for men? There was something artificial about her behaviour which went with her death's-head prettiness. Was the whole carry-on a pose? Whether it was or not, it was impossible to like her.

At home that evening, she heard rustling noises in the garden. Investigating, she found three goats chewing away contentedly at the tender spring shoots of some hybrid musk roses. She rang her neighbours the Tidmarshes, and tried not to sound too shrewish. 'Edward, the goats are in my garden again.'

He made little clucking noises of consternation. 'Oh dear . . . I'm so sorry, I'll come and remove them at once.'

Edward and Wendy Tidmarsh were a couple with an aggressively green life style and extreme left-wing views. They had moved down from London to live a simple, environmentally pure life in a cottage next to the nursery, and had turned its garden into a smallholding. They were awkward neighbours because their earthy way of life involved a loving relationship not only with domestic animals but also with seed-scattering weeds, grey squirrels, moles, and other nuisances which, to the detriment of

20

Archerscroft's seed beds, did not respect property boundaries. Moreover, they had taken to country ways with more enthusiasm than expertise. They spent their lives stumbling from one crisis to the next, and had never mastered the art of tethering a goat. The village regarded them as the best joke it had seen for years, and the gentry ignored them. Celia maintained correct diplomatic relations with them in order to protect the nursery as far as possible from damage caused by their errors of husbandry. They were, rightly, afraid of her, and tried to placate her with gifts of unpalatable goat cheese and vinegary home-made wine.

The Tidmarshes arrived, full of incoherent apologies: the goats had escaped from their sleeping quarters because the padlock on the door of the shed had been inexplicably mislaid. Something of this kind was always happening, but Celia's attempts to make them keep the creatures under control always met stiff resistance from Wendy. Tethering the goats, she insisted, was one of Edward's jobs, but he was very sensitive and insecure, and if he was made to feel inadequate it would put an intolerable strain on their marriage. On one occasion Celia, provoked by this claptrap, had retorted that Edward was indeed very inadequate, as a goatherd if not as a husband. The break in diplomatic relations caused by this remark lasted for several months.

'Don't say anything, please,' Wendy hissed in an urgent aside as Edward ushered the goats back into their quarters. 'I don't want him upset.'

'Very well, but where is that padlock?'

When it had been located in the pocket of Edward's gardening trousers, Wendy suggested a glass of her home-made mead by way of a propitiatory offering. Repressing a shudder, Celia declined and went home.

Next day Bill came into her office and put a slip of paper in front of her. 'Know anything about that plant, Celia?'

Its name was written on the slip: *Schizophragma integrifolium*.

'Yes. A climber with huge white flower heads in July,

21

very spectacular. There's a very well-grown one in the nursery garden at Wakehurst. What about it?'

'Jenny Watson says there was a lovely one in her mother's garden. She thinks we ought to grow it.'

Celia was fascinated; not by what Jenny thought, nor even by the fact that she had nerved herself to communicate her thought to Bill, but by the way Bill had taken notice of it.

'It's a big thing,' she said, 'a bit like a climbing hydrangea, and we haven't got room. It needs a huge wall.'

'Not when it's a seedling in a pot, Celia.'

'But it's not well known and it takes a long time to get it started. Unless people can see it in flower they won't want to buy it. We'd have to grow one to show them and we haven't the wall space. But thank Jenny for the suggestion.'

Instead of going, he hovered for a moment. 'You'd be surprised at how much Jenny picked up in that garden of her mother's. She's a good worker too.'

Celia saw nothing significant about this episode. Suggestions from the junior staff ought to be passed on, and Bill's behaviour to them was perfectly civilized as long as they refrained from drooling over him. Evidently her love-lorn looks had escaped his attention. But she had clearly been trying to impress him with her horticultural knowledge. A few days later she tried it on Celia. Coming up to her in the frame yard, she asked whether Archerscroft had ever grown any of the Mutisias.

'We used to, Jenny, but they're difficult to establish and customers complained when they died, so we gave it up. Why d'you ask, did your mother grow them?'

'She tried twice with *decurrens* but they both died on her, so she put in a *Clematis connata* instead.'

Celia was puzzled. *Clematis connata* was a big rampant thing, much too big for a space intended for a Mutisia. Jenny's mother must have been worried by the bare area of wall and anxious to fill it quickly.

'It must be an interesting garden, Jenny, that your mother made. Where is it?'

'It was near Shrewsbury. But it isn't there any more. Some people bought the house and turned it into a hotel. They built on a huge bedroom wing where the garden used to be.'

Several times during the next few weeks, Celia came upon Bill and Jenny standing close together in some secluded corner of the nursery, in earnest conversation. It dawned on her gradually that Bill had not been blind to Jenny's adoring looks. On the contrary, he had seen them and approved.

This was an unwelcome development. When Bill attached himself to a girl he was blind to her faults and fanatically loyal. He had stuck to Anthea through thick and thin till she turned out to be a murderous psychopath. Since her death his sex life had been a blank, as far as anyone knew. Celia had almost given up hope of his finding a sensible young woman and settling down to engender a row of little Wilkinses.

Jenny Watson was not a sensible young woman. She was a volcano of libidinous hang-ups overlaid with a mass of simpering affectation. Celia hoped fervently that it would come to nothing.

On Friday evenings after the nursery closed she usually invited him in for a drink at the cottage. It was an opportunity for them to put their heads together and review progress away from the pressures of the business. This time he arrived rather later than usual, having changed into his best suit and smothered himself in expensive male toiletries. This was a throw-back to a habit of his during his affair with Anthea.

'Bill, you're looking very smart. What's up?'

'I'm taking Jenny out to dinner.'

Horrors, Celia thought, and cast around for something neutral to say. 'Where are you taking her?'

'Luigi's in Welstead.'

'Goodness, you are pushing the boat out.'

Luigi's was pretentious and expensive. The waiters wore scarlet jackets and brought everything but the salad to the table in flames. Apart from these conflagrations the lighting was discreet. It was an obvious venue for heavy seduction, with expense seen to be incurred.

'Well, I hope you have a lovely evening,' she said and began talking about something else.

When he had gone she took stock. It would have been perfectly easy for him to slink off to Luigi's for his date without telling her. By arriving at the cottage in full breeding plumage and telling her his plans for the evening, he was giving her notice of a serious interest in Jenny.

Celia examined her conscience. Could it be said that she was jealous of Jenny? Not in the crude sexual sense, there had never been even the faintest overtone of sex in her relationship with Bill. She was fond of him and anxious that he should not be hurt, but was that only an excuse, a cover for a possessive interest in him? Was that why she had taken against Jenny?

No. She had disliked Jenny at first sight, before he clapped eyes on her.

Anyway, there was nothing she could do about it. Once Bill had committed himself as far as this, his loyalty syndrome would make him deaf to warnings.

Over the next few days he said nothing to her about the evening at Luigi's and its possible aftermath, nor did she enquire. The news came to her indirectly through Mary Basset.

'You know something, Celia? His nibs took Little Miss Muffet out on the tiles Friday night.'

'Yes. He said he was going to.'

'He tell you he tumbled her into bed with him afterwards, double-quick?'

'No, but I can't say I'm surprised. How d'you know?'

'Oh, it's all round the nursery, Celia.'

Had someone been spying? The gardener's cottage, which Bill occupied, was next to Celia's office and looked out on the frame yard. A sensational development like this in his love-life would be of enormous interest to the whole female staff. Had a horde of giggling women been hiding in the shadows near the cottage to watch the comings and goings? Apparently not. Mary provided a simpler explanation.

'Old mother Parsons, she's been telling anyone who would listen. Would you believe it, she says, her sweet little lodger that's so proper and so considerate, she turns out to have the morals of an alley-cat. She goes out for the evening with that Bill Wilkins, what fornicates like a fire engine, and she doesn't come home, not till seven in the morning.'

This was unwelcome news. 'But Bill doesn't fornicate like a fire engine,' she objected.

'No, but old mother Parsons thinks men do nothing else. It's a pity, if his nibs had slept around a bit he wouldn't have fallen for that silly little box of tricks.'

Jenny was certainly a silly little box of tricks, but she was also in some kind of trouble. One morning, as Celia was walking up the lane from her cottage to begin work, she came on Jenny standing by the gates, in agitated conversation with two men who were blocking her path and preventing her from entering the nursery. She was protesting angrily about something, almost in tears, as they clutched at her to detain her. As Celia approached she managed to tear herself away and enter the nursery.

Instead of moving off the two men stood their ground as Celia approached the gate, and stared at her boldly. One of them was small and dark, with a foxy look and a blue shave. The other, tall and younger, was extravagantly good looking, with luxuriant brown curls and a neat Elizabethan-style beard. They watched her go into the frame yard, then moved off to a car parked further down the lane.

As a conscientious employer, Celia felt bound to send for Jenny and ask if anything was wrong. Did she need help or advice?

'Oh, no, Mrs Grant. It's quite all right, really. I know who they are, please don't bother, I can manage.'

When pressed to say more, she became so agitated that Celia decided to let her keep her tiresome mystery to herself if she wanted to, and sent her back to her work.

Later that morning, the Admiral rang. 'Celia, I've been making enquiries. The RHS say they've no objection to our adding an extra bit of statuary to the design if we want to.'

'But George, we don't want to. Everyone but you is against spoiling the design with extra clutter.'

He decided to sound hurt. 'Celia, my dear. Considering that I'm footing the bill for this exercise, don't you think some slight notice should be taken of my views?'

'Not if you refuse to take notice of everyone else's.'

'Think carefully, Celia. It's my money. I might decide not to stump up.'

Enough of this nonsense, she decided. 'George, don't you dare wave your moneybags at me. If you're determined to mount an exhibition of oversize statuary at Chelsea, you can count me out and find some other unfortunate nurseryman to drive mad. Good morning to you.'

The fallout from this conversation was considerable. During the afternoon she received a flurry of phone calls from people who had been told by Admiral Bond that Mrs Grant had suddenly flown into a fury about nothing and was threatening to leave the society in the lurch.

'Well done, Celia, he's in a right old stew,' commented James Carstairs. 'Leave him to sweat it out, why don't you, till he comes crawling along to apologize.'

All the other callers seemed to have concluded that she must be pacified at once, and that pacification was to take the form of an expensive lunch next day. Unwilling to be bribed with too much overpriced food, she declined sharply, but agreed to meet a delegation from the committee for a snack at a pub out in the country on the far side of town.

Next morning Monica Porter began to fidget at twelve. By half-past she was really agitated. 'Mrs Grant, you haven't forgotten your lunch date?'

'No, why? There's plenty of time.'

'I thought . . . as you're the guest of honour you might want to change.'

Celia looked down at her slacks, which were perfectly

clean, and refused to be intimidated by Monica's aggressively secretarial blouse and skirt. 'Oh, nonsense, we're only going to the pub for a snack.'

'The Three Bells at Fordham, isn't it? They say the restaurant there's quite nice, but perhaps it isn't very dressy.'

It was news to Celia that the Three Bells had a restaurant. Arriving there, she tried hard not to be inveigled into it, insisting that all she wanted was a bar snack. But she was firmly overruled by the delegation, which consisted of Mrs Cadogan as the Admiral's public relations officer, Wilfrid Edgeley, and one of the Admiral's groupies called Charlotte Acton. James Carstairs had evidently been excluded as too pro-Celia and Fred Tunney as too earthy for a restaurant lunch.

Over their prawn cocktails Charlotte Acton delivered what seemed to be a message from Admiral Bond. He was at a loss to know how he had offended Celia and hoped she would reconsider her decision to leave the Garden Society in the lurch. Celia replied that she had no intention of leaving them in the lurch provided the Admiral behaved sensibly, and that he knew this perfectly well.

Mrs Cadogan sprang uneasily to the Admiral's defence. He was a man of ideas, they bubbled up in him all the time, he enjoyed playing with them, but did not intend them to be taken seriously at this late stage in the planning. Everyone nodded solemnly. No one mentioned the Admiral's contention that as he had put up the money for the high jinks at Chelsea he must be allowed to have his fun, but Wilfrid Edgeley hinted that it would be nice if Celia apologized to him.

'Apologize?' she echoed sharply. 'Whatever for?'

Startled out of his skin, Wilfrid explained that he didn't of course mean that she should apologize. What he had in mind was that perhaps she could offer some sort of olive branch.

Ignoring this, Celia summed up by saying that the Admiral was the committee's problem, not hers, and that it was up to them to keep him in order. Having delivered this ultimatum she changed the subject, refused dessert and coffee, said she must get back to the nursery, and broke the party up.

As she pushed her way out through the crowd of drinkers round the bar, a gap opened which revealed an unexpected sight. Sitting at a table by the exit door was Jenny Watson, with an untouched plateful of food in front of her. On either side of her were the two men who had been with her outside the nursery. She was no longer beautiful. Her face was pinched and shrewish and her watery eyes had narrowed into slits, so that she reminded Celia of an angry ferret in a blonde wig. She was arguing with them fiercely, leaving her food untouched. In the intervals of masticating great mouthfuls from their plates, they returned what looked like brief, dismissive answers.

Suddenly Jenny saw Celia looking at her. With a gasp of horror she picked up a menu from the table and held it over her face. It remained there, with Jenny cowering behind it, as Celia walked past her on the way out to her car.

What was all this carry-on about? Jenny was entitled to drink in a pub with whoever she liked, why behave as if she was at a masked ball in eighteenth-century Venice? What was the point of hiding after she had been spotted? Was she afraid that Celia would tell Bill that his virginal dream-maiden drank in pubs with men?

The temptation to say something to him was strong, but had to be resisted. His loyalty would not let him listen. She had no wish to figure as the jealous queen in the fairy story, who tried to wreck the romance between the Prince and his beggar-maid Princess.

Soon after she got back to Archerscroft Jenny reappeared, and slunk past Celia in the frame yard, trying to avoid her eye.

Later that afternoon Celia was in her office when Monica Porter buzzed her on the extension phone. 'I have Admiral Bond on the line. Shall I say you're not available?'

28

'Certainly not, put him through.'

'Ah, Celia,' he boomed. 'I'm glad we're back seeing eye to eye.'

'Are we?'

'Oh, yes, I think so. You're a woman of spirit, you dig your heels in from time to time, I respect that. But you always see reason in the end.'

'Don't you be too sure. If I hear any more talk of guns and storks, I shall become about as reasonable as the witches in *Macbeth*.'

'My dear Celia, there's never been any question of altering your design.'

This seemed to be his idea of an apology. She accepted it only semi-graciously.

When the work-force assembled next morning there was no sign of Jenny. Presently Celia rang her landlady. 'Jenny Watson hasn't turned up for work. D'you know if anything's wrong?'

'There most certainly is.' Mrs Parsons was agog with news. 'I think you've seen the last of that little minx, Mrs Grant.'

'Why, what's happened?'

'Last night just after seven two men came to the house and pushed her into their car and drove her away, and I can't say I was surprised.'

Two

'Two men took her away, Mrs Parsons? What sort of men?'

'I don't know. Just men.'

'A tall good-looking man, quite young, with a beard and a smaller dark one.'

'That's right, Mrs Grant. How did you know?'

'I don't like the sound of this at all, Mrs Parsons. I'll come down straight away and find out more about it.'

On the way to her car she ran into Bill in the frame yard and told him the news.

'Two men?' he echoed angrily. 'What men?'

Celia described them and their odd behaviour.

'Oh, Celia, you should of told me about this before!'

'Yes, I'm sorry.'

'I got to get after her, quick. Suppose I go down there, quiz that naughty old bag.'

'I think it would be better if I went. You're in Mrs Parsons' bad books, as the vile seducer who deflowered innocent little Jenny.'

'Oh, Celia, I never.'

'Maybe not, but she thinks you did. She'd throw you out of the house.'

'Filthy-minded old broomstick, that's what she is.'

'I dare say, but Jenny did spend the night with you.'

'But there wasn't none of that. Jenny's a good girl.'

Wondering what degree of maidenly reticence this might imply, she said: 'Anyway, I still think you'd better let me tackle Mrs Parsons.'

He was in a fever of impatience. 'Mind if I come down with you? Wait till you come out and hear what she's said?'

Celia agreed, and he set off down the lane at a spanking pace, looking grim. Trotting along breathlessly beside him, she concentrated hard on experiencing the anxiety she knew she ought to feel for an employee in trouble. But she could not wholly suppress the thought that Jenny's removal from the scene, however caused, was an unmixed blessing.

The High Street of Melbury, into which they had emerged, had been featured in countless guides and coffee-table books as a beautifully preserved old-world village street; a picturesque jumble of houses and shops, ranging mostly from the sixteenth to the eighteenth century. Celia paused outside Mrs Parsons' small Georgian cottage with her hand on the heavy brass knocker. Bill moved out of sight into the entrance of the half-timbered Elizabethan butcher's shop next door.

Answering Celia's tattoo on the knocker Mrs Parsons, a scrawny old woman dressed shapelessly in black, came to the door leaning heavily on a stick. On seeing Celia she winced, as if further discussion of the previous night's episode was too painful a prospect to contemplate. Having settled Celia down in her tiny living room she launched out into the subject with gloomy gusto. 'It's been a great shock to me, Mrs Grant, a terrible shock, me palpitations were something awful afterwards. I have this heart trouble, you know. Oh dear me, what is the world coming to, I ask you.'

After more lamentation along these lines, Celia asked for details of what had happened.

'It was just after seven, Mrs Grant. These two men came to the house, nicely spoken they were. They asked for her and I called up the stairs for her to come down but she didn't answer and I wondered if she'd gone out without me hearing the door. So in the end I went up and there she was in her room and I told her she'd two visitors.'

31

'The tall, rather good-looking young man with the beard and the smaller dark one?'

'That's right, Mrs Grant. Where was I now? Oh, yes. Presently the two of them came upstairs after me and told her to pack her things and go with them, very firm with her they were. And she started crying and saying she didn't want to go but they said she must and she started screaming and struggling like a wildcat. In the end they had to more or less drag her downstairs into their car, still screeching to wake the dead, you could hear her all down the street. And then they drove away.'

'Did they give any reason for taking her away?'

'I think they were relatives of hers that had heard about how she'd been disgracing herself here, and decided to put a stop to it.'

'Disgracing herself?' Celia echoed.

'Oh dear me yes. She seemed such a nice quiet girl, Mrs Grant, I got quite fond of her. It was a dreadful shock when she let me down so badly.' Mrs Parsons lowered her voice an octave and intoned gravely: 'Men.'

What did this mean? An orgy of promiscuous sex? Or was Bill's offence so dreadful that he had to be referred to in the plural? 'I'm afraid she did get involved a bit with our Mr Wilkins,' she ventured, 'but surely there weren't others?'

'I can't tell, there could have been for all I know. But the way she and that Wilkins carried on was quite bad enough, in the cinema at Welstead one night, you know what they get up to in the back rows there, and out with him all night the next. Disgraceful! She should have been ashamed of herself, no wonder they came and took her away.'

'You're sure they were relatives of hers? They said so?'

Mrs Parsons did not seem certain of this at first, but decided in the end to be quite sure. 'Yes. The young one said he was her brother, and the other was . . . an uncle, I think it was, but I couldn't hear properly what with Jenny screaming and cursing and saying she didn't want to go with them.'

'You didn't at any time suspect, Mrs Parsons, that these

two men were not relatives of Jenny Watson's but were kidnapping her for some criminal reason, and that you ought to have done what you could to help her?'

'No! Of course not!' cried Mrs Parsons in a sudden outburst of vehemence. Clearly, that uncomfortable thought had occurred to her, and she had been fighting down guilt about it ever since.

Asked to describe the car they were driving, she said all cars looked alike to her, but she thought it was white or cream. 'I didn't notice, she was making such a shocking fuss.'

Outside in the street Bill was waiting eagerly for Celia's report. She outlined what Mrs Parsons had told her.

'Was they really her relations, d'you think?' he asked.

'Goodness knows. According to Mrs Parsons, they said they were. But if they did she obviously didn't believe them, and now she's choking down remorse because she knows she ought to have tried to interfere.'

'So the silly old bag didn't tell you nothing useful.'

'No. She couldn't even describe their car, except that it was white or cream.'

'There's others can. What with Jenny hollering and the two guys cursing at her, people came to their windows and looked out. The butcher next door has a teenage son that's a car buff, he says it was a white two-door BMW with a damaged front wing. He even noted the number, PEN 22. One of them personalized numbers you can buy.'

At his suggestion, they walked round the corner to Tunney's garage in the hope that the BMW, being a thirsty car, might have been filled up there. It had. The pump attendant remembered it, having noted the contrast between an expensive personal number plate and damage to the wing which should have been repaired before it began to rust. Disappointingly, the driver had paid with cash, and not with a credit card which would have given a clue to his identity. But the pump attendant remembered him well. He was small, wiry, and dark, and had spoken with a pronounced Irish accent.

The next step, clearly, was for Celia to drive into

Welstead and report the incident at police headquarters there, but the idea filled her with distaste. Welstead police station was still a place of horror to her. Three years ago it had been the scene of her battle to prove Bill's innocence in the teeth of police obstruction and hostile local opinion. But she resigned herself to the inevitable, and refused Bill's pressing offer to come with her. He would probably lose his temper and start shouting if the force failed to produce Jenny at once.

As she drove the six miles into town all the butterflies in her stomach rose in revolt. But she took a firm grip on herself and went into the doom-laden building. To her relief the desk officer and the detective constable who took down the details of her story were both new to her, and there was no sign of the detective inspector who had accused her of trying to pervert the course of justice.

Detective Constable Burton looked young and inexperienced. He noted down her story with no obvious signs of hostility. 'And these men claimed to be relatives of the young woman?'

'So the landlady says. Whether they are or not is another matter.'

'Very well, madam. We'll look into it, and check that car number on the computer.'

She got up to go. 'By the way, does Inspector Ferris still work here?'

'No, madam. He left the force some time ago. I understand he helps out in a pub in Brighton.'

It was said with a relish which suggested that Ferris had not been popular. She left the building feeling a lot better.

Back at Archerscroft she found Mary Basset wondering if a customer who had ordered *Schizostylis* 'Sunrise' should be offered 'Admiral Byng' as a substitute because 'Sunrise' was out of stock.

'Yes. He won't know the difference,' Celia decided absently, for her thoughts still ran on Jenny. An uneasy query that had nagged at her subconscious for some time was bobbing about urgently on the surface.

34

'Mary, about Jenny Watson. How old would you say she was?'

'Hard to say.'

'Not a school-leaver waiting to go to college?'

'Never. Is that what she told you?'

'Yes, but there were times when I thought she looked a lot older.'

'You can say that again, Celia. Twenty-five at least. Perhaps nearer thirty.'

Shocked by her own ability to shut her eyes to the obvious, Celia went back to the office and rang St Elizabeth's Girls' School in Bath. It admitted to having two sisters called Watson on its books, neither of them called Jennifer. Neither of them had left at the end of the summer term.

Less surprised than she had expected by this intelligence, she rang Wye College, which confirmed after consulting its file of applicants for places in the autumn that it had no application from a Jennifer Watson, and Cannington Agricultural College in Somerset also drew a blank. Determined to do the job thoroughly, she rang a woman who ran a small nursery in the outskirts of Shrewsbury.

'Mrs Woodcock? Celia Grant, d'you remember me? I had the stand next to yours at the Great Autumn Show.'

To judge from the vague noises at the other end the woman did not remember, but Celia pressed on. 'I hope you don't mind, but I need some information. D'you know of a rather good garden somewhere in the Shrewsbury area which got built over when the house was sold and turned into a hotel?'

This proved too much of an earful for Mrs Woodcock to absorb at one hearing. When it was fed to her in short takes with pauses between, she still seemed bewildered, but disclaimed knowledge of any such garden.

'You're sure? I'm told the woman who owned it went in for rarities, especially climbers, Schizophragmas and Mutisias and the species clematis, things like that. I thought she'd almost certainly have had dealings with you.'

35

In tones which suggested that she thought Celia slightly mad, Mrs Woodcock repeated that she knew of no such garden in the Shrewsbury area.

Celia tried two other nurseries with the same result, then, to make doubly sure, rang a very grand one whose managing director was influential in the affairs of the Royal Horticultural Society and a fellow-member of hers on Floral Committee B.

'Sorry, Mrs Grant, if this was as good a garden as you say we'd certainly have heard of it, and I don't know of any house with a worthwhile garden that's been turned into a hotel in the last few years. What's the trouble, a bad debt?'

'No, an applicant for a job who's told me a pack of lies.'

'Oh, well, that happens. Nice to hear from you.'

Bill was dividing ligularias on a bench in one of the two houses and potting them up. She approached him in fear and trembling and told him of her discoveries. 'And I think this means that she isn't a teenager, in spite of what she said. She looked quite a bit older to me.'

For a moment Bill froze, stiff from shock. Then he jabbed viciously with his knife at the ligularia clump in front of him, but said nothing. She waited. After a time he said, 'OK, Celia,' in a dead voice which conveyed that he wanted her to go.

It was lunch time. The refrigerator at her cottage yielded the remains of last night's quiche, but she had no appetite. She was deeply sorry for Bill, but also furious with him. He kept women at arm's length in case they developed designs on his chastity, and consequently knew nothing about the species. Then suddenly, as in the case of Anthea, he would put a girl up on a pedestal. But Anthea and Jenny had one thing in common. A pedestal was the last place where they belonged.

During the afternoon she was on her knees in a seed bed when Monica rushed out of the office and pounced on her. 'You haven't forgotten, Mrs Grant, that you have an appointment to have tea with Mrs Fortescue at Kenlake Manor?'

She had forgotten, but would have died rather than admit it to Monica. Affecting a leisurely saunter till she was out of sight, she dashed up the lane to the cottage and changed out of her grubby jeans. Only slightly late, she turned in at the wrought-iron gates of Kenlake Manor.

The first hundred yards of the drive ran between banks of hugely overgrown rhododendrons, planted by some Victorian owner of Kenlake, and seemingly neglected ever since. The Fortescues wanted her to do something about them. She had agreed, but had yet to decide what could be done.

Beyond the rhododendron avenue the drive ran across beautifully landscaped open parkland towards the house, a largish late-Georgian mansion with a pillared entrance porch. The door was opened to her by one of the Filipino servants who were the mainstay of the establishment when Mrs Fortescue was there alone. When her husband was in residence, they were reinforced by a number of large muscle-bound men who travelled with him everywhere. They were obviously his body-guards, for like many ultra-rich men he lived in fear of kidnapping or worse. But he had decided for some reason that his wife faced no such dangers, and needed only whatever protection the Filipinos could provide.

Margaret Fortescue was waiting for her in the graceful oval drawing room overlooking the gardens on the far side of the house. She was a dark-haired woman who dressed quietly and wore little or no make-up, but turned out to be surprisingly beautiful when one looked at her attentively. Celia admired the quiet dignity with which she accepted the role of dowdy stationary wife to a husband in perpetual and glamorous motion, who circled the globe to control his business empire. If the gossip columns were to be believed any spare time he had was spent 'escorting' appetizing female members of the international jet set.

'Ah, Mrs Grant, thank you for coming,' she said. 'There's trouble in the long border, come and look.'

She led the way out on to the terrace, and down the steps to the border below it which Celia had laid out for her three years ago. It had been maturing nicely, and she had been rather pleased with it. But though it was early in the season, ugly gaps were beginning to show.

'The drought last year did more damage than I thought,' said Margaret.

Together they reviewed the casualties: a pieris, most of the hydrangeas, a kalmia, and two magnolias. None of them showed any sign of rising sap. It was too late to put in even container-grown replacements. That would have to wait till the autumn. Celia agreed to provide big herbaceous plants to fill the gaps over the summer.

The area of shrubs on the far side of the lawn had fared better, but there were gaps there too. When she had made notes of what needed replacing, they went back into the drawing room for tea.

After several hesitations and false starts Margaret raised a subject which clearly embarrassed her: the rejection of her application to join the Melbury Garden Society. 'You're on the committee, aren't you, Mrs Grant? What on earth happened?'

'Oh, it was a stupid business. Admiral Bond took it on himself to turn down your application without consulting anyone.'

'Because he'd quarrelled with Jason?'

'I'm afraid so, yes.'

'But is it for him to decide?'

'No, but they all truckled under. He always waves his moneybags at them if he doesn't get his own way. You see, he's paying the expenses of this Chelsea extravaganza, and they're afraid he'll leave them with the bill if they stand up to him.'

'If there's ever a problem with money, Mrs Grant, Jason and I would be very happy to oblige.'

'That's very kind of you, but all seems to be well for the moment.'

'Good. We don't want to make any more bad blood in

38

the village if we can help it. Let me know, though, if there's more trouble.'

'How very generous. After what happened, I wouldn't blame you if you cut the village off with a shilling.'

'I'm not upset about it, not really. It was Jason who wanted me to join, I wasn't keen because I thought something like this might happen. He rang me soon afterwards from Tokyo and asked me about it and I had to tell him. He was furious, as I knew he would be.'

'Oh, dear. Has he calmed down at all since?'

Margaret frowned. 'The trouble is, he's very protective about me. I expect I'll have a difficult time with him when he gets back.'

'Must we expect ructions?'

'I'm afraid so.'

'Do try to shield us from the wrath to come.'

She looked uneasy. 'I'll do my best.'

Celia drove back to Melbury full of foreboding. Margaret Fortescue was a nice woman. She had brought the subject up to deliver a warning. She would do her best to calm her husband down, but she did not expect to succeed.

Back at Archerscroft, the work-force was preparing to leave. Mary Basset stopped at the gate for a word with her. 'Been up to Kenlake, have you?'

This seemed to be the prelude to something.

'Yes. Why?'

'That Mrs Fortescue's a dark one, Celia. You need to watch her.'

'Goodness, Mary. What d'you mean?'

'Got a fancy man, she has. Goes up there when Mr Fortescue's away.'

'Oh, nonsense. What about the servants? They'd tell her husband.'

'They're not supposed to know. He comes late at night and leaves his car in the park somewhere and she lets him in. He's gone again while it's still dark, and no one any the wiser.'

'Mary, I don't believe a word of this.'

''S true though. My Paula had it from someone that knows.'

Mary's daughter Pauline served behind the bar at the Red Lion, a listening post for village gossip. According to Mary, one of the other barmaids was carrying on with a Filipino manservant at Kenlake who frequented the pub on his days off. 'Smashing to look at, and randy as a he-goat,' said Mary. 'He seen it happen twice, and he told her.'

Celia was not convinced. Why would a servant be awake at that hour? She dismissed the story from her mind as the sort of fable a Filipino trying to seduce a barmaid might invent to tickle the appetite of his prey.

Moving round the nursery in the next few days she detected tension in the air. Word seemed to have gone round that Mr Wilkins was in one of his moods and best kept away from, and the gossips knew what the mood had been caused by. Uncertain what his low-flashpoint temper might lead to, Celia hesitated to call him into conference when, late one afternoon, Detective Constable Burton from Welstead arrived to report his findings about Jenny's abrupt departure. But she decided in the end he had a right to be there.

'I had a word with this Mrs Parsons, madam,' Burton reported. 'And she's quite clear that the two men described themselves as relatives of Miss Watson, a brother and an uncle.'

'She's lying,' Bill interrupted. 'She's only saying that 'cos she feels guilty. She knew Jenny was being kidnapped and she ought to of interfered.'

Burton addressed himself firmly to Celia. 'This puts the police in an awkward position, madam. We're very reluctant to get involved in disputes within a family.'

'That's not what this is,' Bill barked.

'We've no evidence that it's anything else, Mr Wilkins. What we've got here is a very young girl at odds with her relatives. We're supposed to steer clear of domestic quarrels unless there's a risk of actual bodily harm.'

'If you won't do anything about it, I will,' Bill stormed.

40

'You traced that car? I'll have something to say to whoever it belongs to. Whose is it?'

'I'm sorry, I'm not at liberty to tell you.'

'Why the hell not?'

'We're not authorized to release information from the
computer to members of the public.'

'I'm not a member of the public, I'm her boyfriend.'

'I understand how you feel, Mr Wilkins, and I know
you'd like to rush off and pick a quarrel with the young
woman's relatives. But I'm sure you'll see that the police
can't be a party to that.'

This was too much for Bill with his low flashpoint. He
insisted furiously that this was not a family row, that
Jenny would probably be murdered, and if the police did
nothing to prevent it he, Bill Wilkins, would see that
they were crucified for negligence. The young detective
constable received this tirade with admirable calm, said
he would keep an eye on the situation, and withdrew with
his dignity intact, leaving Celia convinced that he would
go far in his career.

For the rest of the week Bill remained sullen and unap-
proachable. When he came to the cottage for his usual
Friday night drink and chat, Celia decided that the subject
of Jenny could not be avoided.

'Listen, Bill. How much did she tell you about herself?'

'Not much. She talked mostly about poetry, she knew
lots by heart.'

'She must have said something about her background.'

'Only about how she'd been unhappy in Canada, on
account of how her stepfather treated her rough. Before
that in England she was OK, her mum and dad hadn't
split up and she loved that garden of her mother's.'

'Which didn't exist. And she doesn't have an application in for a place at Wye or Cannington and the school
in Bath that she says she's just left has never heard of
her, and anyway she's much too old to be a school-leaver.'

'OK, Celia, OK.'

'No, it's not at all OK. You've been had for a mug and

41

I'm sorry. But do you have to go round with a face like thunder and terrify the staff into fits?'

'It's not just on account of Jenny. I got a wisdom tooth nagging me.'

'Then get it attended to, for Heaven's sake.'

'OK, but don't you nag me too. I got an appointment in Reigate Monday.'

They talked for a time about other things. When it was time for him to go she said: 'Try not to think too much about Jenny. I honestly don't think she's worth it.'

'OK, Celia,' he said despondently and went out into the night.

Nursing his aching tooth over the weekend, he wondered if she was right. Should Jenny be condemned to the compost heap like a seedling of some newly crossed hybrid that turned out to have an ugly habit and flowers the wrong colour? He had never come up against anyone like her before: brainy, quick with her hands, clued up about rare plants with difficult names, into literature, poetry and all that, things he had never thought about before. But she had no self-confidence at all, and looked to him all the time for comfort and shelter. As she saw how much he liked her, she had blossomed out like a winter iris in the February sun and that had really set him off. But now the whole thing had been blown sky-high, she had told lies about herself. Who were the two kidnappers? Was she perhaps in fear of her life, did she need to hide from them? Was that why she had faked a false identity, to avoid being tracked down? There were moments when he managed to believe this. It was reasonable for her to have lied to Celia in her job application. But why did she have to feed a false identity to her lover, lying naked in his arms? Why had she not come clean?

Driving into Reigate on the Monday morning to be relieved of his aching wisdom tooth, he decided firmly to give her the thumbs down. He parked, and walked along the crowded High Street to the dentists' beside a tailback of slow-moving traffic, trying not to remember all the nice things about her. His tooth was in agony, but so was his mind. Forcing himself not to weaken, he stared blindly at the line of cars overtaking him slowly, then snapped suddenly into alertness. The car which had just passed him was a white two-door BMW.

And its number was PEN 22.

He ran after it and – yes, there was a girl in the back, behind the driver and the severe-looking woman sitting beside him. It was Jenny. As the car halted at a pedestrian crossing, he caught up with it and rapped on the window beside her.

Jenny bounded up in her seat, torn between delight at seeing him and anguish at being trapped in the rear seat of a two-door car. Clenching her fists, she began battering at the head of the woman sitting in front of her, who blocked her exit. The woman turned, gripped Jenny's wrists and began twisting them. At the same time, the driver slewed round in his seat and struck Jenny a vicious blow in the face. She cringed down towards the floor of the car, trying to protect her head with her arms.

The pedestrian light changed to green and the BMW moved on. Bill ran after it, but it soon gathered speed and left him gasping and frustrated on the pavement.

He had been wrong about Jenny. She had been hiding from danger, there was some secret in her life so awful that she could not reveal it, even to him, and now she was being brutally maltreated by her kidnappers.

On the way back to the nursery he called in at Welstead police station and reported his sighting of Jenny to Detective Constable Burton, who noted everything down impassively, but saw no reason to alter his private opinion, which was that Bill had lost his head over a girl whose family thought him unsuitable.

Back at Archerscroft Bill stormed into the office and told his tale of woe to Celia. 'I seen her. In Reigate. They got her in that car.'

When he had calmed down enough to tell her the story, she asked if he had reported it to the police.

'Yes, but they won't do nothing.' For a time he stood

frowning in front of her desk and clenching and unclenching his fists. 'Oh, Celia. Can't you put your thinking cap on and come up with something? We can't go on like this.'

So saying, he retreated towards the seed-beds wearing a grim expression which warned his fellow-workers to keep clear.

He's right, Celia thought, we cannot go on like this. In his present state Bill was no use to the nursery, his bad temper was upsetting everyone. There would be no peace till the basic question about Jenny had been settled. Was she the innocent victim of evil men or a worthless minx? Much as Celia disliked the prospect of yet another trip down the Miss Marple trail, she could see no alternative to finding out the truth. But where was she to start?

She had always been puzzled by Jenny's deftness at pricking out and potting on, which seemed unlikely to have been acquired at any private garden, however large and busy, and anyway the garden near Shrewsbury did not exist. That sort of skill was much more likely to have resulted from intensive practice in a commercial nursery.

And where, if not at the Shrewsbury garden, had Jenny learnt to talk knowledgeably about unusual plants? At a professional nursery which specialized in them? Possibly.

After some thought she reached for the *Plant Finder*, a guide to plants not available in ordinary garden centres. It contained details of specialist nurseries and semi-amateur gardeners who could supply them. Jenny had mentioned three such plants: a Schizophragma, a Mutisia, and a species clematis – what was it? Oh, yes, *Clematis connata*. Assuming that she had come across all three at some nursery specializing in unusual climbers, it should be possible to identify the nursery with the help of the *Plant Finder*.

Schizophragma integrifolia was quite widely available. Only clematis specialists seemed willing to bother with *connata*, a rampant clematis which produced miserable little pale yellow bells. The rest of the trade probably shared Celia's view that it was rather boring. Only four firms dealt in the difficult mostly frost-tender mutisias, and of these only two listed *decurrens*. A hasty search through the pages of the *Plant Finder* showed that the same nursery also grew a few species clematis, including *connata*. If Jenny had worked in a nursery it had to be this one, so she rang it.

'Martindale Nurseries.'

Coupled with the name, the voice with its hoarse undertone of smoker's cough rang an immediate bell with Celia. 'Goodness, that's not Peggy Martindale?'

'Well it must be, there's no one else here capable of answering the phone. Martindale nurseries consists of me and a mentally retarded old age pensioner. Anyway, who are you?'

'Celia Grant. Celia Mackenzie that was.'

'Oh, my God, a voice from my dim girlhood past, how are you?'

Peggy Martindale had been the comic turn of Celia's year at Wye. They had lost touch since but Peggy was an excellent plantswoman and according to gossip in the trade she tended to launch small and unprofitable nursery businesses in the gaps between her disastrous marriages. After they had brought themselves up to date with each other's news, Celia put her question. 'Peggy, have you ever employed a girl called Jenny Watson?'

'No, dear, I can only afford to hire teenage criminals and mental defectives.'

'A very blonde girl and appallingly shy, but very competent at the potting bench. Watson may not be her real name.'

'Ooh, her! Goodness, yes, that does ring a bell. But she called herself Jean Williams when she was here. Gave me the creeps, a cross between a Barbie doll and a very slimy mermaid, never spoke above a whisper.'

'That's her. Wanting a temporary job till she could take up a place on a horticultural course in the autumn?'

'No, dear, having to take refuge from the manager of that big nursery near Swindon, because he got passionate and tried to rape her, though how you set about raping

45

a mermaid I can't imagine. Of course I smelt a rat, but you have to ignore the smell of rats when you're operating on a shoestring like me, and she said she was a beginner and only wanted a starvation wage, so of course I hired her.'

'And then what happened?'

'Nothing much, except one morning she wasn't there. I wasn't very surprised because I'd never believed in the nursery manager and his lust. I simply enjoyed having her while it lasted because I was sure she'd go off as soon as whatever fix she was in had been sorted out.'

'So how long was she with you?'

'About six weeks, I suppose. What made you think she might have worked for me?'

'It's a long story. Peggy, could I come over tomorrow and go into this in more detail?'

'Of course, I shall be fascinated to hear.'

'And may I bring my head gardener? He's part of the long story, I'd better warn you about that now.' She sketched in the details. 'And now he's in a fog of frustrated love and bad temper, upsetting the whole staff and snapping everyone's head off, all because that tiresome little minx mewed at him like a half-drowned kitten. Aren't men infuriating sometimes?'

'All men are infuriating all the time, dear.'

'Anyway I shan't get any sense out of him till I've discovered why little Miss Mischief keeps popping up and telling lies about herself and disappearing again. That's why I'd like to bring him along to hear your bit of the saga.'

'Ooh, leave it to me, dear. By the time I've finished blackening her she'll be the whore of Babylon and no mistake.'

'Goodness. Did she exercise her wiles on someone at your end?'

'No, Celia dear. There's only my mentally retarded pensioner, and he thinks sex is something that dogs and cats do.'

'Don't lay the whore of Babylon on too thick, or Bill will decide that we've made it all up to put him off her.'

Celia set off next morning, with Bill eager and agog beside her. She had told him only the bare fact that she had identified a previous employer of Jenny's, and expected him to shut his ears and sulk when presented with the full and rather discreditable story. Following Peggy's directions she turned off just beyond Salisbury on to a winding by-road in the valley of one of the tributaries of the River Avon. Martindale Nurseries proved to consist of a rickety notice-board, a tumbledown cottage, and two plastic-covered tunnels, bounded by a loop of the river. The whole place had a downtrodden unprosperous look, which did not surprise Celia. A nursery on soil full of lumps of chalk, bounded on three sides by a chalk stream, and with a water supply which must be heavily alkaline, could hardly expect to prosper.

They found Peggy in one of the tunnels, with an elderly man working beside her. The plants, climbers at the seedling stage or supported on canes, looked surprisingly healthy, a tribute to her skills as a plantswoman.

'Hullo, dears,' she cried. 'One moment and I'll be with you.' She gave some kind but firm instructions to her pensioner in a told-to-the-children voice, then advanced towards them and said: 'Let's go up to the cottage, shall we?'

At this point she noticed Bill's astonishing good looks and gave a sharp double-take. 'He's gorgeous,' she murmured to Celia as they walked up the path. 'We can't let him throw himself away on that tedious little harpy.'

The living room of the cottage was tiny, with the ashes of a dead wood fire on the open hearth. It also served as the office, to judge from the mounds of paper which had to be removed from chairs before they could sit down.

'Gin, dears?' Peggy enquired, then with less emphasis: 'Or coffee?'

Over the coffee, which seemed to Celia better suited to the time of day than gin, she began her recital. To Celia's relief she was being studiously neutral, and told

47

the story of Jenny's alleged escape from the threat of rape without letting the slightest tinge of disbelief creep into her voice. She praised Jenny's efficiency as a worker, and said how sorry she had been to lose her after so short a time.

'About when she left,' said Bill. 'Did she seem worried then, as if there was people after her?'

'No dear, I don't think so. But I was out most of that day, making a delivery. I wouldn't necessarily have noticed.'

'There wasn't any men hanging around the place on the look out for her?'

'No. At least, wait a moment, I seem vaguely to remember . . .' She screwed up her eyes for a moment in thought. 'Yes, it comes back to me now. At the beginning of that week, it must have been, two scruffy-looking chaps drove up in a car, asked if I could sell them some bedding plants. I said, "Sorry no, I don't grow them, try one of the garden centres or a supermarket in Salisbury." That didn't put them off though, they said, "As we're here can we have a scout round, see if anything takes our fancy?" I didn't like the look of them one bit, so I went with them in case they pinched anything. They squinted at one or two of the labels and said "That's nice, very unusual," but I could tell, they couldn't have told a Mutisia from an African marigold. In the end they went away without buying anything, and I forgot all about them.'

'And where was Jenny all this time?' asked Celia.

'That was odd too, now I come to think about it. I looked for her when they'd gone but she was nowhere to be seen. In the end I realized that she'd locked herself into the loo, which is outside round at the back. She was in there so long that in the end I went and knocked on the door to find out if she was all right. She said she was and after a bit she came out.'

'But you didn't connect the two things?' said Celia. 'It didn't occur to you they might have come to look for Jenny?'

'Not at the time, no. I didn't believe in the rape story, and anyway neither of them looked imposing enough to be the business manager of a large nursery with rape on his mind.'

'What did they look like, then?' said Bill quickly.

'Let me see. One of them was quite young, rather dishy with a fancy beard, trimmed like Henry VIII's. The other was a little blue-chinned runt of an Irishman.'

'It's them lot again, Celia,' said Bill.

She nodded. 'Peggy, what made you think he was Irish?'

'The way he spoke, I suppose. The sort of voice the Irish put on to sound more attractive.'

'How about the car?' Bill asked.

'White. Rather swanky. I remember thinking the two of them didn't belong in that car.'

'Registration number?'

'Sorry, no. I didn't notice. But I did notice that someone had given it a bash on one of the wings.'

This, it seemed, was all the information Peggy Martindale could provide. But there was one other possible source.

'Her landlady might know something,' said Celia. 'Where was she living while she worked here?'

Peggy thought. 'I'm not sure, she arrived every day on one of those phut-phut scooter things, second-hand, it was always breaking down. Wait a minute, though, she gave me her home address when she arrived, and oh yes, she wrote to me from there after she left asking me to post her her last week's wages. Rather cheeky, I thought, after leaving me in the lurch.'

'Did she say why she'd left?'

'Having to look after her invalid mother, I think she said. Anyway, all this means that I must have an address. I wonder if I kept it.'

She pulled open a desk drawer brimful of paper and began burrowing in it. Celia and Bill watched in suspense as she sorted through invoices from seedsmen, personal letters, clippings from newspapers, bank statements, and

49

miscellaneous rubbish. Finally she found Jenny's letter, stuck to a greasy grocery bill. 'Here we are, dears! Keeper's Cottage, Hayter Down, near Amesbury.'

'Where's that?' Bill asked.

'Ten miles north of here. Off you go and good luck to you.'

As they sped towards Amesbury, Bill was in high spirits. 'There, Celia, I told you! There's these two dodgy jokers hot on her trail, she has to keep moving, but they always find out somehow where she's gone off to. No wonder she tells these stories about herself to put them off.'

Celia cursed inwardly. Peggy's information had reinforced his obsession instead of starting the cure. 'I wonder what the real story is,' she murmured.

'Oh, Celia, that's what we got to find out.'

Three

Keeper's Cottage came in sight on a bleak ridge overlooking the empty downland of Salisbury Plain, with a belt of trees behind it giving meagre shelter from the wind. As the car bumped towards it along a grass-grown track, Celia began to suspect that it was derelict. The neglected garden was full of scruffy bushes and brambles, the paint was peeling and the windows looked blank. There was no sign of life.

'Jenny'd never live in a dump like that,' Bill decided, 'not all by herself in the middle of nowhere. It's a wrong address she gave to put them jokers off.'

Nevertheless, it seemed sensible to investigate. Repeated knocks on the door were not answered, but a dustbin round at the back contained the wrappings of several takeaway meals, and an empty milk carton with a sell-by date which had expired three days ago.

'Somebody must be living here,' said Celia. 'But they're away at the moment. Shall we be very wicked and break in?'

For the first time for a week, he grinned. 'Sure, Celia, why not?'

The catch on the kitchen window gave him little trouble. He climbed over the sill and unlocked the back door to let her in.

The kitchen was clean and tidy. It smelt of the paraffin used in the cooking stove. There was no refrigerator. A small larder contained nothing perishable.

A door leading to the rest of the house was ajar, but resisted attempts to open it fully. The obstacle proved to

51

be a dilapidated armchair, lying upside-down against the door. Beyond it in the living room a table and a standard lamp had been overturned and a pottery vase lay smashed on the floor.

'Someone been fighting in here,' Bill decided.

A bookshelf attracted Celia's attention. Most of the books dealt with green issues, from the depletion of the ozone layer to the dangers involved in using chemical pesticides in gardens. While Celia looked through them, Bill opened a walk-in cupboard to one side of the chimney breast. In it were half a dozen roughly made notice boards fixed on stakes, ready to stick into the ground. He turned one of them round to see what was on it. 'Oh Celia, come and look at this!'

Fixed to the notice board with drawing pins was a paper target, ready for target practice. Indeed, someone had been practising already. Several of the other targets were riddled with bullet holes.

'It doesn't add up,' Celia grumbled. 'If you're so green that you can't bear to kill aphids, what d'you want with firearms?'

At Bill's feet was a cardboard box, which he opened. It contained a stack of leaflets. He picked up one of them, glanced at it and handed it to her. 'Here's your answer to that.'

The leaflets had a bold heading in green:

COMMUNIQUÉ
from
THE FIGHTERS OF THE GREEN FRONT

The Fighters of the Green Front announce that they intend to use all necessary means, including direct action, to arrest the pollution of the environment by agricultural and horticultural interests which damage it for reasons of commercial profit.

- Peat is a finite, non-renewable natural resource. Wetland from which it is extracted can never regenerate, and the peat-extraction industry is

52

destroying a unique habitat which is the only one in which certain specialized species can survive. There is no justification for pretending that part of a wetland can be despoiled while the rest is preserved as a Site of Special Scientific Interest, because extraction of peat affects the water table of the whole area, including the SSI. Two and a half million cubic metres of peat are used annually by commercial and amateur horticulture. The destruction of our few remaining wetlands must stop, and we intend to see that it does. We consider firms which extract peat or sell it to the public to be legitimate targets and liable to attack. So are commercial growers who use it. Even amateurs who do so should not consider themselves immune.

- Over half our rivers are seriously polluted by run-off into them of chemical fertilizers used on crops. Manufacturers and sellers of these fertilizers are therefore designated legitimate targets.

- We also declare a ban on the manufacture, sale, and use of harmful horticultural chemicals, particularly persistent ones based on organochlorines and broad-spectrum indiscriminate killers containing thiobendazole. Manufacturers and sellers of such drugs, and of others which we may name from time to time, will be ruthlessly eliminated. Amateur gardeners who are misguided enough to use them must also expect reprisals.

- Manufacturers, sellers, and users of any of the above must consider themselves liable to attack by operational units of the Front:

YOU HAVE BEEN WARNED

Celia turned the leaflet over. Its back was closely printed with a list, under their brand names, of horticultural chemicals considered by the Front to be mutagenic, carcinogenic, harmful to wildlife, or otherwise noxious.

'Well, well,' she commented. 'A lot of their criticisms

53

are quite sensible, but do they really intend to underline the message by letting off bombs?'

'I dunno, but they're practising shooting.'

'Horrors. Is violence the right way to tackle this sort of problem?'

'The animal liberation people think so, Celia. What a thing for Jenny to get herself mixed up in.'

'Bill, how is she mixed up in it?'

'She knows too much, and they're afraid she'll talk.'

'But she doesn't talk. Why not? If she disapproves, why doesn't she go to the police? Instead, she keeps quiet and gets herself one job after another by telling lies. But they always find her. Why?'

'I dunno, Celia.'

She looked round the room. 'If there are targets there ought to be guns. Where are they?'

A thorough search yielded none. But in a cupboard in the kitchen they found a metal box with military-style markings on the khaki paint of its lid. In it was a carton of ammunition and also some curious assemblies of electrical wiring, with batteries attached. Bill put out a hand to pick one up.

'Don't!' said Celia sharply. 'Don't touch them, I don't like the look of them at all.'

He drew his hand back. 'Nor me neither.'

'And Peggy Martindale says one of those men is Irish.'

They looked at each other for a moment in horror.

'Oh, Celia, we better get the police here double-quick.'

But she hesitated. 'Let's look round the rest of the house first, shall we?'

A bathroom, grimy from lack of recent use, contained a dirty towel and some toilet articles. Beyond it at the end of a short passage was a half-open door. It led to a bedroom which was in disorder. The furniture was all intact, but the bed was unmade, drawers gaped open, and there were women's clothes littered about the room. 'Jenny's?' Bill asked.

Celia began picking over them. 'I expect so.'

'Was there a fight in here too, then?'

'No. This is what a room looks like when someone has packed in a tremendous hurry.'

'So she packs in a hurry and knocks thing over next door in her panic to get out.'

'Very well, but when? She wasn't here recently, unless she escaped from the two men you saw parading her round Reigate and came back here. But to judge by the dustbin, someone was in here a week ago. Why didn't they clear up a bit?'

'I dunno, what d'you reckon?'

She picked up a dress from the bed and held it up against herself. 'I'm sure Jenny wouldn't be seen dead in a thing like this.'

It was a dismal black cotton shirtwaister with a niggly little pattern in white, the sort of dress that no one under sixty would buy. 'And it's not even clean,' she added.

Picking over garment after garment, she found fault with several of them which were the wrong size for Jenny, or not clean, or in need of repair. 'These aren't Jenny's clothes.'

'Then whose are they?'

'I don't know, I need to think. Give me one of the leaflets out of that box, and let's get out of here.'

Under her instructions he removed all traces of their visit. Then he locked the back door from inside after her and climbed out of the window he had broken in through.

'There'll be a police station in Amesbury,' he said. 'We better go there.'

'No!'

He stopped in his tracks. 'What d'you mean, No?'

Celia found it hard to say. Instinct had warned her that all was not what it seemed at Keeper's Cottage. Apart from that knowledge, her mind was in turmoil.

'We're not going to the police,' she managed. 'Not yet, till we've thought a bit.'

'But it's urgent. There's Jenny to consider. What is there to think about?'

Instead of answering she started back towards the car, then halted. 'One minute. I want to check something.'

55

She turned aside and approached the front door. A straggling, unkempt pyracantha grew against the wall beside it. She began searching among its twigs, and presently found what she was looking for on a nail driven into the wall behind it. The turmoil in her mind resolved itself. 'Ah, I thought so. They even left us a key in case it didn't occur to us to break in.'

'Celia! You gone crazy or something?'

'No. I realize now. Everything inside there was an exhibit, specially fixed up for us to find.' She shivered. 'This place gives me the horrors. Let's get away from here and I'll try to explain.'

But he would be furious at what she had to tell him. As she drove off down the grass-grown track in silence, she tried to devise some way of softening the blow.

'Come on, Celia,' he urged. 'What's all this, then?'

There was no help for it, the confrontation had to come. She pulled off the road into a lay-by. 'You see, Bill, she made it much too easy for us.'

'Who did?'

'Jenny. She says she learnt her skills in her mother's garden near Shrewsbury. When I find that the garden doesn't exist, I suspect that she's worked at a commercial nursery. When I wonder which one, she tells me. She mentions three rarish climbing plants, including a recently introduced and rather dreadful clematis* that hardly anyone stocks. The *Plant Finder* lists only one nursery that stocks all three. We go there, and get given the address of that cottage, where we find a tableau specially set up for our benefit.'

'You're out of your mind, Celia, why would she do that? You're saying Jenny's been leading us by the nose. I'm not having that, you've no right.'

'Listen for a minute before you fly off the handle. Jenny's behaviour from the beginning has been very odd. She arrives and tells me a pack of stupid lies, knowing that I can prove her a liar the moment I lift the telephone. Why?'

---

* Celia was being rather unfair to *Clematis connata*, which is deliciously scented.

56

'I've told you. To put them two dodgy villains off of the track.'

'If that was it, any intelligent ten-year-old could have invented a more watertight cover story. No, I was meant to find out that she'd lied and get interested. Then she got you into a hot and bothered state of love, to make sure I took the thing seriously and started following up the clues. But for you I wouldn't have made the effort. You bullied me into it because she'd got you into a state about her. What actually happened during your fabulous night of love?'

'I told you. Jenny's a good girl.'

'What does that mean? Probably that she let you play about as much as you liked provided you didn't actually put it up her. No, don't interrupt. In my young days girls who behaved like that used to be vulgarly known as prick-teasers. It's the oldest trick in the world for keeping a man on the hook.'

'Celia! It's not like you to talk dirty.'

'I'm sorry, but we've got to face facts. When her lies have got me mildly interested and you hot and bothered about her, two men appear and behave threateningly. Their very noticeable car has a number plate so easy to remember that no genuine kidnapper in his senses would dream of using it. They then purport to carry her off. We rush after her in hot pursuit, and trace her to Peggy Martindale's. Realizing that Peggy keeps a very disorderly office, Jenny has written to her after she left with a reminder of her address, in case Peggy's mislaid it. Thanks to this sensible precaution Peggy is able to direct us to Keeper's Cottage. We rush off there hot-foot and feast our eyes on horrifying evidence that it is the headquarters of a sinister organization planning terrorist activities in defence of the environment. We think we've been very clever, but in fact we've simply been following the trail of clues in a treasure hunt designed to lead us there.'

'No, Celia. Why would anyone want to do that?'

'To make us believe that this bloodthirsty green organization actually exists. I can't think why, it must be some kind of practical joke. But whoever's behind this suddenly realizes that we've come looking for traces of Jenny, so he ought to provide some. So he buys a collection of clothes at a jumble sale and strews them around the bedroom. Being a man, he doesn't realize that some of them won't pass muster.'

'Celia, what you're saying doesn't make sense. Look. I'm in Reigate, walking down the main street, and what do I see? Jenny in that car, it just happens to be there same time as me. She sees me and tries to make them let her get out, so they give her a bashing. That was for real. You can't say different.'

'Yes, I can, because I don't believe in extraordinary coincidences. What's the obvious route from the main car park in Reigate to that dentist's above the art shop? Along the High Street. So anyone who knew the time of your appointment would find it perfectly easy to drive up alongside you as you walked along it and stage that little vaudeville act.'

'Celia, you're raving. How would they know when I was due at the dentist's?'

'Someone told them.'

'Why?'

'Because you'd got a lot less keen on Jenny and something had to be done to get you interested again.'

'Oh come on, Celia. Who's telling them all this?'

'Well, Monica Porter made the dentist's appointment for you.'

'You're not saying she gave them a tip-off!'

'I can't prove it, but who else could it have been? And here's another extraordinary coincidence that I don't believe in, also involving Monica. You remember, Jenny and her two men friends staged one of their little performances for my benefit at the Three Bells in Fordham. Monica knew I was going there to lunch there, she tried to bully me into dressing up as if it was the garden party at the Palace.'

'But you've no call to put the finger on Monica. You've no proof.'

'I know, but I've always been puzzled about her. She played down her qualifications when she applied for the job, and it turns out that she's much too high-powered for us. Why did she throw up her post in London, whatever it was, and move down here?'

After digesting this in silence, Bill started to argue back. 'Celia, you're saying Monica got herself hired so she and Jenny and those two men could act silly with us. Why would she want to?'

'Someone could have argued her into it. Someone who hates me and wants me to look a fool. Lots of people know that I have this fatal bug of curiosity which makes me rush off and start detecting at the drop of a hat. It could be that I'm meant to follow up all these clues and dash off to the police station with a hectic story about a terrorist movement in favour of organic vegetables. Then they come out in the open and say it's a hoax and I look a proper Charlie.'

'Who's doing all this?'

'Goodness knows. I've a lot of enemies in the village, because of that business three years ago. Ann Hammond, the Tunneys, the Berridges, old Colonel Templewood. They've never forgiven me for having unearthed that awful story.'

'You don't believe this, Celia. You can't. Who is there in the village would plant clues all across the country? Who knows enough about the *Plant Finder* and all that? Who's going to organize Monica into taking a job that's beneath her so she can spy on us? Boozy old Colonel Templewood? Fred Tunney or Chris Berridge from the garage?'

'I don't know!' Celia wailed. 'No one in the village, perhaps. I just know we're being tricked, I feel it in my bones.'

Simmering with frustration, he tried another tack. 'Another thing, Celia. Be honest now. Would you of rushed half across England after Jenny if it hadn't been for me getting interested in her?'

'Probably not.'

'So you only did it because I'd got the hots for Jenny and started being a bit dodgy and difficult at work, and you thought you'd cure me by clearing the mystery up. Right?'

'Yes, I suppose so.'

'So how did whoever's behind this scheme of yours know I'd fall for Jenny and set you off detecting?'

'Oh, I hadn't thought of that.'

'Well, you should of, Celia. Everyone around the place knows I'm fussy. Till now I've never laid a finger on any of the girls at work, and I slap them down if they get silly ideas, so how could these dodgy people of yours be sure I'd get interested in Jenny?'

It was the first really telling argument he had produced. Filled with self-doubt she drove out of the lay-by in silence and started towards home. Presently Bill attacked again. 'What do they call it when someone starts thinking people are plotting against them, whispering behind their backs? You need to watch out, Celia.'

'Stop it, Bill. I'm not going mad. I'm just in a muddle. I don't know what to think.'

'I know what I think. You know you should go to the police, tell them to go to that cottage, get after Jenny, find out what those electric gadgets are. But you won't do it, because you've always been afraid of the police, you think you'll not be believed.'

'No. It isn't that.'

'Then turn off into Amesbury. There must be a police station there.'

'No.'

'There, what did I tell you? You're scared to.'

'I'll go to the police tomorrow, but I've had an idea that I want to try out first.'

'There you go. Excuses.'

'Stop it, Bill, leave me alone. I want to think.'

After a time he began attacking her again furiously, but she choked him off and they drove home in stony silence. By the time they reached Archerscroft she had convinced herself miserably that he was right, she was suffering from delusions of persecution. Reason insisted that it was absurd to suspect anyone in the village of organizing such an elaborate plot against her, and she could think of no enemy further afield to blame it on. But she distrusted reason, the voice of instinct insisted on being heard. There was only one way of silencing it; by putting her improbable theory to the test.

When she arrived at the office next morning she told Monica to cancel an afternoon date with her hairdresser. 'Such a nuisance, I've got to go all the way back to Wiltshire.'

'Oh, what a pity, Mrs Grant. You didn't have any luck there yesterday?'

'Well, I found out where Jenny was living but she wasn't there. I went inside to make sure and I stupidly left my reading glasses there. I'll have to go back and collect them.'

Was it imagination, or was Monica looking interested and rather pleased?

When she told Bill where she was going, he had only one thought. 'You going to tell the police?'

'I expect so. But I want to go back to Keeper's Cottage first.'

'Why? Want me to come with you?'

'No. One of us ought to be here.'

'Then mind you tell the bluebottles all about it.'

She drove back to Wiltshire in the rain, thankful not to have him as a silent, disapproving presence beside her. Beyond Andover the sun broke through, and when she turned into the track leading to the cottage it and its shelter belt of trees stood out in brilliant sunshine against the pile up of ominous thunder-clouds behind it.

She parked on the grass in front of the cottage and got out. She was shivering a little, and wished she had accepted Bill's offer to come with her. Nothing seemed to have changed since her last visit, but this time she was nervous. Had Monica tipped off the performers about her coming, and if so what sort of vaudeville act had they laid on?

It looked as if she had, something had changed. Three

imposing motorcycles stood half hidden among the scrub to one side of the cottage. People were moving about in the shelter belt of trees. They were armed, and in the field on the far side the targets she had found in the cottage had been set up on their posts. At a word of command, they raised their guns and fired.

As the rattle of rifle fire broke out, Celia decided that this was no place for a lady, alone in the wastes of Salisbury Plain with an armed gang. She scurried back into the car, and was about to start the engine when a grey-haired man came out of the trees, shouting and gesticulating at her. He was dressed in black leather, replete with brass studs, death's-head medallions, and dangling fringes. He ran up to the car and rapped on the driver's window. She wound it down.

'What the bloody hell are you doing, poking your nose in here?' he barked. 'Fuck off before you get shot.'

'Goodness, how alarming. Is that a threat?'

'Don't be so fucking stupid. You can hear, there's firing practice going on, it's dangerous. Off you go, you're trespassing on private land.'

But the firing was in the opposite direction, there was no real danger.

'I'm sorry,' she said, 'but I'm here because an employee of mine hasn't turned up for work, Keeper's Cottage is the address she gave. I've come to see what's happened to her.'

'Balls. There's no one living here. The place is empty.'

'Are you sure? Her name's Jennifer Watson.'

He frowned suspiciously. 'Whoever told you got it wrong. Now get off my land before you get hurt.'

It was a threat, and intended to be taken as one. She started the engine, turned and set off towards the main road. He stood watching her, a black-clad figure posed theatrically in front of the deserted cottage and the thundercloud. Watching him in her rear mirror as she drove away, she was elated. Her suspicions were correct. On a man that age the black leather costume with brass fittings amounted to fancy dress and the rude words sounded like an act. The rifle fire, the shadowy figures in the wood, the whole episode smacked of theatre. It had to be a 'happening' specially arranged for her benefit after a tip-off from Monica.

Then a reaction set in. Why would anyone go to such lengths to make a fool of her? Perhaps Bill was right, to suspect Monica was pushing conspiracy theory too far. It was just a coincidence that the cottage was empty one day and a hive of belligerent activity the next. She distrusted coincidences, and there had been quite a number of them lately, but they did happen. If genuine terrorists were caught at firing practice in a wood, they might well warn off an intruder so energetically that it looked theatrical.

The police had to be alerted. On the way into Amesbury, she worked out what to say. There was no question of mentioning her suspicion of a hoax. If she did, the sniggers of barely concealed disbelief would reduce her to a nervous wreck. She would confine herself strictly to the facts. Well, fairly strictly. There would have to be one or two small adjustments.

In Amesbury she choked down her stomachful of butterflies and marched boldly into the police station. It was too small an outpost to have a permanent CID presence, so she confessed herself to a friendly station sergeant. She had been worried, she said, about an employee of hers called Jennifer Watson, who had been forcibly removed from her digs by two men purporting to be relatives of hers. Having found out her permanent address from a previous employer, she had gone to Keeper's Cottage and found no one there. But the key was on a nail by the door, so she had gone inside and found broken furniture, a bedroom in disarray, and targets, ammunition, and devices which could be detonators in a cupboard. She had also found terrorist leaflets threatening violent activity in defence of the environment and had removed one of them which she produced from her handbag and handed over.

In a necessary adjustment of the truth, she implied that this inspection of the interior of the cottage had taken place on that very day, quite early in the morning. Then, she said, she had driven part of the way home. Wanting to consult the map, she had missed her reading glasses. Concluding that she had left them at Keeper's Cottage, she had gone back to look for them and found what appeared to be terrorists engaged in firing practice.

The sergeant looked impressed, and said he would have the matter investigated at once. 'And if we find your glasses, madam, we'll forward them to your home address.'

'Oh, how kind, but that won't be necessary. So stupid of me, I found them just now under the seat of the car.'

She drove back to Archerscroft with a sense of civic duty well done and was attacked by Bill as soon as she set foot in the office. 'You tell them?'

'Yes.'

He was going to add something, but she stopped him with a gesture. The door of the outer office was open, Monica could overhear. 'Let's go outside.'

Out in the frame yard he turned on her angrily. 'You still putting the finger on her?'

'Yes, and I was right about her.' She told him about the performance that had been laid on for her at Keeper's Cottage.

'How d'you know it wasn't for real, and you just happened along on the same day?'

'This was one coincidence too many.'

He frowned impatiently. 'You say anything to the police about them funny ideas of yours?'

'Of course not, you know why. If there's anything in it, they can find out for themselves.'

'They'd be better employed looking for Jenny,' he retorted, and turned away.

That evening Admiral Bond rang her at home. 'Ah, you're back. I tried to get you earlier. Listen, my dear, something rather urgent has come up.'

'Horrors, what's happened?' she asked, fearing some new twist to the Chelsea imbroglio.

64

'Well, you know I've bought Baker's Meadow?'

She collected her thoughts. 'Is that the big field behind your house? I didn't know it was for sale.'

'The old man who owned it died. I've bought it from the executors. Can't have some filthy developer moving in and putting up nasty little villas along the bottom of my garden. What I wanted to ask you is, have you heard this nonsense about there being a public footpath across it?'

'No. Is there a footpath marked on the Ordnance Survey?'

'I think there may be, but it hasn't been used for years. Wouldn't you say it had lapsed?'

'Goodness knows, the law on footpaths is very tricky.'

'But I'm going to let the field for grazing. We can't have herds of people tramping across it. I can count on your support, can't I? I'm raising it at the Parish Council meeting tomorrow night.'

Celia had been elected to the Council after taking a prominent part in a campaign to deliver the village from the threat of a hypermarket. What was now being suggested, she realized, was that she had better vote the right way over the footpath or else. She mumbled something non-committal and cut him off.

Opening the refrigerator at breakfast time, she was confronted by an alien plastic box containing, she suddenly remembered, a present from the Tidmarshes of some goat cheese. It had been there for over a fortnight, and must by now be even more revolting than when she had closed the box hastily after sampling it. She threw the cheese away and washed out the box, so that she could return it on her way to work.

As she opened the Tidmarshes' rickety gate, she tried to devise a form of words which would combine gratitude for the gift with discouragement of any tendency to repeat it. The smallholding looked as untidy and depressing as usual. Even the cats looked discontented. Her knock on the door of the cottage was answered by a fat woman she had never seen before, dressed in a shapeless smock.

'Ai'm Annabel Johnson,' she said and put a coy finger

65

to her prominent chin. 'Don't tell me, let me guess. You're . . . Mrs Grant, is that raight?'

Celia admitted that this was so, and asked if the Tidmarshes were away.

'Oh yes, Edward and Wendy have been gone quaite a time, they're at a conference. Ai'm from Friendly Cousins. We look after peoples' homes and animals while they're away. Only organic, as Ai'm sure you realaize. If the people are inorganic, we won't touch them.'

Celia knew all about Friendly Cousins. They were called on to mind the cottage and livestock on the frequent occasions when the Tidmarshes wanted to attend environmental conferences of one kind or another. They came in all shapes and sizes. Some of them attacked the Tidmarshes' chaos with the determination of brisk new brooms, others ignored it and behaved as if on holiday. Annabel Johnson was new to Celia and inspired instant dislike. Her prominent chin, large nose, and staring grey eyes added up to some kind of menace, and her wispy fair hair looked far from clean. Invited to come in for a chat, she shivered. It was like being invited into the doom-laden gingerbread house by the witch in Hansel and Gretel.

'Thank you, but I have to go to work. Another time, perhaps.'

'Well, yes. Another taime maight be better. Edward and Wendy are dears, but they left the plaice in chaos and I haven't had the strength to do much taidiying up yet. Looking after the laivestock is as much as Ai can manage.'

Celia withdrew, wondering why she had disliked the woman so much. She could see no reason for it, but the feeling amounted almost to a physical revulsion.

After the day's work, the prospect of the Parish Council meeting faced her. She had been tempted to send an apology to avoid having to declare a position about the Admiral's footpath. But she had strong views on the recycling of garbage, which was also on the agenda, and she decided to attend.

Ann Hammond, the doctor's wife, was the chairperson.

For many years she had behaved as if she had a God-given right to run the affairs of the village, and had been in firm control of everything in it except her own collapsing bun of thick grey hair. But her position had been challenged lately on two fronts. The Admiral had political ambitions, and was supported by a few malcontents at Ann Hammond's rule who did not realize how muddle-headed he could be. At the other end of the political spectrum, the workaday population of the council houses kept up a ground swell of revolt against the domination of the village by the gentry. Two cautious solicitors and three commuters from the new executive estate on the edge of the village manoeuvred uneasily between these rival factions.

Celia's position on the council was unenviable. Because of the crisis over Bill three years ago she was at daggers drawn with Ann Hammond as well as with the Tunney family's village mafia, which was massively represented on it. Caught between these two hostile forces, she foresaw that a third war-front would open up unless she supported the Admiral in his nonsense over the footpath.

When the agenda item about the handling of refuse came up, her proposal for saving and recycling newspaper was dismissed as 'airy-fairy' by Arthur Tunney and as 'out of the question on grounds of expense' by Ann Hammond. The Admiral murmured something to the effect that a method involving less expense might be found, but was slapped down at once from the chair and subsided, having only made this gesture in support of Celia because he hoped for her support over his pathway.

This came up next under 'any other business'. The immigrant commuters, always the fiercest opponents of any threat to the old-world nature of the village, protested loudly that the pathway was traditional and must be preserved.

'Surely it's marked on the Ordnance Survey?' said Ann Hammond crisply.

The parish clerk, whose business it was to be informed about such matters, confirmed that it was.

'In that case,' said Ann, 'there's nothing to discuss.'

67

She was right. Like most villages, Melbury was surrounded by a network of forgotten or half-forgotten footpaths used in past ages by farm labourers walking to work. As recreational footpaths most of them served no useful purpose, and had been allowed to lapse. But they still existed as rights of way in law, and abolishing one of them involved horrendous legal problems and great expense.

Nevertheless, Admiral Bond began to bluster. This was ridiculous. The pathway served no useful purpose, there was a more direct route along the public road. Surely a right of way which had not been exercised within living memory could be said to have lapsed, it stood to reason. He was sure Mrs Grant would agree with him.

Before Celia could damn herself eternally in his eyes by prevaricating, one of the solicitors intervened. 'I think perhaps I should say something before we go further into this. Am I right in thinking that the footpath in question crosses Baker's Meadow?'

'Yes, Mr Armitage,' said Ann in a tone which rebuked him for not paying proper attention.

'In that case I don't quite understand why Admiral Bond describes himself as the owner, since Baker's Meadow was sold yesterday to someone else.'

The Admiral laughed easily. 'Oh, dear, how these stories get around. I'm afraid you've been misinformed.'

'I don't think so. You see, my firm acted for the purchaser.'

The Admiral made little choking noises.

'Well, if there's no other business,' said Ann with unconcealed relish, 'I declare the meeting closed.'

'No!' roared the Admiral. 'Who is this mysterious purchaser? I insist on knowing. It's a monstrous piece of bad faith, the heirs had agreed to sell to me.'

'There's no mystery about it,' said Armitage. 'We were acting on behalf of Consolidated Developments Ltd.'

'A developer!' cried the Admiral in horror. 'Madam Chairman, I want to propose an emergency resolution, to the effect that any application by this developer to build on Baker's Meadow will be turned down flat.'

'Hear, hear,' said the three commuters in unison.

'We cannot take an attitude to a planning application till one has been submitted to us,' said Ann firmly. 'And now I really think we should close the meeting.'

'One moment, please,' the Admiral growled. 'Who owns this wretched firm?'

'Consolidated Developments,' said Armitage, 'is a member of the Hanbury-Fortescue group of companies.'

'Fortescue! You mean, that international crook up at Kenlake Manor has bought Baker's Meadow? And is going to build houses on it?'

Celia gasped. This was what Margaret Fortescue had been warning her about. Her Jason, outraged by the insult to his wife, was having his revenge.

Four

'That man is a blot on the good name of humanity,' Admiral Bond muttered angrily as he and Celia walked up the lane together to their respective houses. 'Fortescue isn't even his real name.'

'So you told me.'

'One doesn't expect a jumped-up refugee from the gutters of the East End to possess the rudiments of decency, but you'd think the solicitors acting for old Mr Baker's heirs would be men of their word. As for Fortescue, I shall use his guts as garters before I'm through.'

'George, nobody likes to see his wife humiliated. I'm not surprised at him trying to get his own back.'

'But the documents were all ready, the witnesses were standing by, everything was going to be signed, sealed, and delivered tomorrow. Who whispered a tip-off into that unspeakable cad's ear, so that he could creep in at the last moment with a better offer? That's what I would very much like to know.' He brooded for a moment. 'I could cheerfully disembowel whoever told him.'

By the time their ways parted at his gate, everyone from his own solicitor to the village postman had come under suspicion.

For the next few days Bill went on fretting, and had to be restrained from ringing Amesbury police station to ask if they had found Jenny yet, and if not why not. Celia hoped callously that Jenny and everything connected with her could now be consigned to oblivion in Wiltshire, but an unexpected phone call shattered her hopes.

'Mrs Grant? My name's Wilberforce, I'm a policeman.

70

It's in connection with a statement you made at Amesbury police station. I'd like to come and put a few questions to you if I may.'

'Oh. Yes, of course.'

'Could I call on you early this afternoon?'

She hesitated. Everything they said would be overheard by Monica in the outer office through the flimsy partition.

'Could we meet somewhere else? At police head-quarters in Welstead, perhaps?'

He agreed, and they fixed a time. The next problem was, whether to take Bill with her. It seemed only fair in view of his fixation about Jenny, but she decided against it. If Jenny had not been found he would complain and disrupt the proceedings with his bad temper. Feeling slightly guilty, she went alone. The bad vibes of the police station were dispersed to some extent by a friendly greeting from a desk sergeant whose face was vaguely familiar. 'This way, Mrs Grant. The superintendent will be with you in a moment.'

But the small bare room she was shown into held horrible memories of the interviews in it three years ago. The feeling of doom gathered round her again. After a minute or two Superintendent Wilberforce joined her; a tall man in his fifties with a slim figure in a well-cut grey suit. The outer corners of his eyes and mouth drooped downwards, giving him a strangely lugubrious expression. It seemed entirely appropriate for a senior policeman to look exactly like a bloodhound. He introduced himself and his cheerfully round-faced assistant Sergeant Padstow in a frighteningly formal tone.

'I'm sorry you had to come all the way from Wiltshire to see me,' she said, tense with nerves.

'Not Wiltshire, actually. London. The Special Branch.'

So the thing was being taken seriously. For some reason that made her feel even worse.

They sat down, and Sergeant Padstow opened his notebook.

'We're very grateful for your statement, Mrs Grant,' said Wilberforce. 'It was very clear and accurate. When

71

the local people got to Keeper's Cottage the motorcyclists had left, but everything else was exactly as you described. But one point puzzled us. According to information from other witnesses, gunfire was heard from there as early as ten in the morning. So we don't understand how you managed to go there during the morning without seeing them, and examine the contents of the cottage at leisure, although according to you they were still there when you went back to look for your glasses, which you thought wrongly that you'd left there.'

The butterflies in her stomach rose. 'Oh dear. I'm afraid the statement contained one or two lies.'

The Superintendent raised one eyebrow. 'Really? Then perhaps you would be good enough to tell us the truth now.'

The cool mockery was worse then being scolded. 'Yes. Of course,' she stammered. 'You see, my first visit, when I went into the cottage, was on the previous day, before the motorcycle people got there. When I'd seen what there was to see I went home, and came back the next day.'

He frowned, but in what looked like puzzlement rather than anger. 'So you delayed for twenty-four hours before you contacted the police. Why?'

'Because I wanted to think things out first. You see, I had an idea, an idiotic one, I realize that now, that the whole thing was a hoax, to make me look a fool.'

Sergeant Padstow let out a startled grunt, and the Superintendent seemed to be suppressing signs of amusement. The atmosphere in the room had changed, but she could not decide what the new atmosphere was.

'Do go on, Mrs Grant. You thought it was a hoax. Why?'

Haltingly, she took him through the steps of her reasoning: Jenny's peculiar behaviour at Archerscroft, the improbable coincidences, the carefully planted series of treasure hunt clues leading her to Keeper's Cottage, and the sinister exhibits she had found there.

'But next day you went back there? Using your lost reading glasses as an excuse?'

'Yes, I knew I had them with me all the time.'

'And the motorcyclists were there then?'

'Yes, and after that I went to Amesbury police station.'

'I don't quite understand this, Mrs Grant. What prompted you to go back to the cottage first?'

'Oh, horrors, I'm afraid you'll think I'm paranoid. I had an idea, you see, that someone who knew about our movements, mine and my head gardener's, was masterminding the thing and arranging for the coincidences to happen in places where we were going to be. My secretary, Monica Porter, seemed to be the most likely person because she usually knows where we're going, so I thought I'd test out my idea. I told her I was going back to Keeper's Cottage, thinking she might arrange for a coincidence to happen there for my benefit.'

The signs of amusement had become more pronounced. Her recital was getting an even worse reception than she had feared.

'So you actually fed the woman what the spy thrillers call a barium meal?' said Wilberforce. 'And watched it popping out at the other end?'

Struck only by the coarseness of the expression, she plunged on. 'Yes, but afterwards I realized that coincidences do happen and the motorcyclists could have been there without Monica having anything to do with it. So I kept quiet about my idea when I got to the police station in case they laughed up their sleeves at me, which is what you two are doing now.'

They sobered up at once. 'I'm sorry, Mrs Grant, you've got us quite wrong. You're not paranoid, you've got it absolutely right. You've come to exactly the conclusion we would have reached on the evidence, and you've taken the same action that we would have taken, to test the thing out.'

Relief flooded over her. 'You mean, you believe it's a hoax?'

'Yes. There have been three episodes of the same kind, apparent caches of sinister warlike exhibits to which we or members of the public were led by a carefully arranged coincidence. There was one in disused lead workings on the Yorkshire moors and one in a holiday cottage at Burnham-on-Sea and the third was in a lock-up garage in . . . where was it, Sergeant?'

'Willesden, Super.'

'Oh, yes, and in all three places there were leaflets like the one you handed in, usually in packets ready for distribution.'

'But who's doing all this?' Celia asked.

'We don't know. Motorcycles and helmets to hide the face seem to be constant features. We think it's probably the same people travelling round, like a small theatrical company on tour.'

'What an extraordinary carry-on. What's the point?'

'Publicity. And to make the thing look bigger than it is.'

'I'm sorry, I don't understand.'

'Look, Mrs Grant, I wouldn't normally discuss a security matter of this importance with a member of the public. But I got a bit of background on you from the local force here before you arrived. Everyone from the Superintendent down gave you a tremendous write-up. They tell me that apart from taking charge of a murder investigation and preventing a miscarriage of justice, you put an end to the career of an odious little inspector whom everyone loathed, and got him turned out of the force.'

This new insight into police thinking at Welstead left her speechless.

'You're an unusual member of the public,' Wilberforce went on, 'so I'm going to talk to you very freely, on the understanding that everything I say is confidential.'

'Of course.'

'For weeks the whole environmental movement has been buzzing with rumours to the effect that green extremists are planning to launch a campaign of violence against firms which produce or use persistent garden chemicals, or peat, which they say is destroying the wetlands from which it is extracted. We've had quite a few phone calls, some of them anonymous and others from environmentalists opposed to violence. They give different versions of the organization's name, but they all agree

74

on one thing: it intends to mount a terrorist outrage at the Chelsea Flower Show in London next month.'

'Horrors,' said Celia.

'Yes. You're in the business. You realize what that means.'

Celia certainly did. In the crowded conditions at Chelsea a bomb hidden behind a few dahlias could kill several hundred people. And with over a thousand exhibitors bringing in the wares for their stands the security problem would be horrendous. Even plants in containers would have to be uprooted while the soil under them was searched.

'I agree, it's a gruesome prospect,' said Wilberforce. 'But they'd be mad to try it, however fanatical they are about the environment. A massacre at Chelsea wouldn't do much to popularize their cause. You've probably heard it said that terrorism is theatre. What matters is the impact on the public, and it looks as if someone has hit on a way of getting the impact without having to produce the terror.'

'So you're sure the whole thing's a hoax? That nothing will happen?'

'We're not sure, I wish we were. Those gadgets you found at Keeper's Cottage were detonators all right. Not very sophisticated ones, but what worries us is they're a type the IRA was using about five years ago. That means the organization we're dealing with is in touch with some very sinister people.'

'Which suggests that the threat is real?'

'Not necessarily. The things were probably planted there by hoaxers wanting to make their threat look more credible, but we can't be sure of that. And even if we were sure it was a hoax, we'd still have to take it seriously, if only because after all these rumours the whole environmental movement will be in uproar if we don't mount a tremendous security operation at Chelsea. When the media see that they'll begin to ask why, and the RHS will have to issue some kind of statement. So one way or another the hoaxers will get their publicity.'

75

'What do the organizers at the RHS think about all this? They're not proposing to cancel?'

'So far they're showing no signs of caving in.'

'Goodness, what a mess,' Celia murmured, imagining the tearing of hair that must be going on among her friends and colleagues at the Society's headquarters in Vincent Square.

'Yes, but we're not beaten yet. We've got three weeks before Chelsea to catch these people and stop their nonsense, and thanks to you we've several new lines of enquiry to follow up. Tell me about this secretary of yours, what's her background?'

Celia described Monica Porter's suspiciously recent arrival at Archerscroft with suspiciously superior qualifications for the job there. 'She gave a very good reference from a firm of solicitors in the City, and said she was leaving them because she wanted to live in the country for health reasons. But she seems perfectly healthy to me, aggressively so in fact.'

'Right, we'll get her investigated straight away. But she's a recent arrival in the district, you say. What guided her to you as a target for the hoax? Someone with local knowledge must have put her up to it.'

'Yes. The village has attached this Miss Marple label to me because of that case three years ago, and a lot of them bear me a grudge because of what I found out. My first thought was that one of them had targeted me to make me look silly so that they could take me down a peg.'

'Whoever it was underrated you, didn't they?'

'Some of my enemies probably think I'm not very clever.'

'If that's so, they don't know you very well. Perhaps only by reputation.'

'My goodness, that gives us a horribly wide field. The population of Melbury is three and a half thousand, not counting the surrounding district.'

Sergeant Padstow showed signs of wanting to say something.

76

'Yes, Harry?' Wilberforce prompted.

'I was wondering, sir, if the information could have come from someone in the district who's prominent in the green movement.'

'Yes, how about that, Mrs Grant?'

Celia hesitated. 'Oh, horrors. There's one possibility, a couple called Tidmarsh, who have a smallholding right next to the nursery. They're fanatically green and very left-wing. But their smallholding's a mess and they can't even make a drinkable home-made wine, one shudders to think what a conspiracy run by them would be like. It's probably unfair of me to mention them to you, they're such obvious suspects that I must be wrong.'

'Even so, I think we should interview them.'

'You can't,' Celia remembered. 'They're away at a conference.'

'Ah. What sort of a conference?'

'I don't know, but they usually go to green ones, and shower me with pamphlets afterwards.'

'You don't know their forwarding address?'

'No, but I can probably find out from the woman who's looking after the place for them.'

'Please do, if you can manage it without arousing too much curiosity. The other person we're very interested in is of course this girl who calls herself Jennifer Watson.'

'Alias Jean Williams from when she was working at Martindale's, and probably alias a lot of other things as well. Let me see, what can I tell you about her? She was very experienced and quick at handling plants, she's obviously worked at some time in a commercial nursery. But I think she must also have trained as an actress. The masquerade she put on at Archerscroft was very convincing. I don't think a person without acting experience could have pulled it off.'

'Ah, that's very helpful. What did she look like?'

Celia did her best to describe Jenny's repulsively waxen blonde beauty. 'If she is an actress her picture will be in the casting directories. Would you like me to look through one, in case I recognize her?'

'That would be very kind. I'll get hold of one and post it to you.'

Next they discussed the supporting cast, Jenny's two 'kidnappers'. Celia thought the tall young man with the beard could also be an actor, but was less sure about his dark companion with the blue shave. 'He was small and fierce and ratlike, he'd have looked ridiculous on the stage. And I hope this doesn't frighten you too much, but two witnesses say he had a pronounced Irish brogue.'

Wilberforce looked grave. 'Do they indeed? Who are they?'

'A pump attendant at the garage in the village here, and Peggy Martindale when they visited her nursery garden. I told you about that.'

'Yes. Could you give us Miss Martindale's address?'

Wilberforce noted it down, then asked about the car that the Irishman had been driving. 'I think my head gardener gave the police here a description of it, and the pump attendant at the garage may be able to tell you more. It had a damaged wing and there was something very odd about its number plate.'

'Good. We'll get on to that aspect too. I think that's as far as we can get for the moment. Here's the phone number of our report centre in London, it's manned day and night, so if anything new happens, or if you have any fresh ideas, do ring.'

Fearing eavesdropping by Monica Porter if he called her at the office, she gave him her home number and asked him to ring her there out of office hours if the need arose. Then she left, fortified by smiles from the two policemen at the desk which she no longer thought contemptuous and derisive.

Archerscroft was shut by the time she got back. She decided to call in at the Tidmarshes on her way home and get their address from their stand-in. A ghetto-blasting radio was on when she arrived at the door. The fat woman was just as repulsive and much less welcoming than before. Leaving the radio on, she explained that she had

78

something on the stove, and kept Celia standing outside while she went in to write down the address of the commune where the conference was being held.

Back home, Celia phoned through the address to the London number that Wilberforce had given her. But as she came in she had picked up a note in Monica's writing from the mat, and when she opened it her investigating euphoria left her and she came down to earth with a bump. Admiral Bond had telephoned, Monica reported. There had been an important development which he wanted the committee of the Garden Society to consider urgently. Could they all meet at his house that evening at eight?

Celia's heart sank. Presumably the 'important development' was yet another flash of quarter-deck insight about Chelsea. He would have to be slapped down firmly, and she arrived at the meeting full of bad-tempered determination. But the reality was even more infuriating. He had decided to launch an appeal for funds to 'save Baker's Meadow for the village'. It was to be laid out as a cricket and football pitch, with swings and slides for the children in one corner. He wanted the committee's backing for his scheme. 'And I thought it would be a nice gesture if we all put a bit of money into the kitty to start the ball rolling.'

The three commuters from the new executive estate approved loudly, since anything was preferable to having more houses like their own built in the village. The Admiral's groupies stirred uneasily at the thought of having to part with money. Fred Tunney pointed out that the field was sloping and too small for cricket, whereas the existing cricket ground was flat and spacious. 'And we need more houses in the village,' he added, 'to stop the young people leaving.'

While the Admiral fumbled for an elegant way of saying 'not in my back yard', Celia burst in fiercely. 'George, you really are the limit. You've brought us here on false pretences to discuss a sudden brainwave of yours which has nothing to do with the Garden Society, and anyway is a complete non-starter. You've grossly insulted the wife of the man who's bought that field, and he's not going to sell it on to you at any price. It's within the village envelope and there's no planning reason why it shouldn't be built on. I agree with Fred, it would be nice if some of the houses were affordable by first-time buyers, but I'm not wasting any more time on this. I propose that we end the meeting without further discussion.'

'And I second that,' said Barbara Bradshaw.

'Oh, come now . . .' the Admiral began.

'Without further discussion,' Celia repeated. 'Come on, let's vote. Those in favour?'

James Carstairs and Fred Tunney raised their hands at once. Wilfrid Edgeley put his up half-way and looked round the table to see what the others were doing. When the three groupies also voted in favour, he made up his mind and joined them. 'Seven in favour,' said Celia. 'Against?'

Mrs Cadogan abstained. Only the commuters supported the Admiral, who was livid with fury. 'I am not angry,' he shouted. 'Just deeply saddened and – yes, bewildered to find so little loyalty and devotion to the interests of the village. Well, I think I had better withdraw from the meeting and leave you to go on making your plans for Chelsea, including of course the new financial arrangements you'll have to make.'

With that, he marched out of the room.

'Oh dear,' said Wilfrid Edgeley, 'shall I go after him and tell him we didn't mean it?'

'No,' said Celia. 'He'll have to be told something quite different. Mrs Fortescue, who is a customer of mine and a very practical woman, told me the other day that she and her husband would be willing to fund us at Chelsea if other sources dried up.'

Fred Tunney laughed. 'That'll bring the old bully to his senses.'

'However,' Celia went on, 'she'd prefer not to make the bad feeling between them and George any worse, so she wouldn't put forward the offer unless she was sure he means what he said just now and won't change his mind. So let's all go home and leave Mrs Cadogan to go and find out if his decision is final.'

As they trooped out of the room, Mrs Cadogan gave Celia an enigmatic smile, to which Celia responded with a broad wink.

While she was having breakfast next morning, Wilberforce came through on the telephone. 'Have you opened your post yet? There's a letter from me with some photos in it.'

She collected her letters from the doormat. An official-looking envelope contained two pictures of Jenny, a full face and a profile.

'Recognize it?' he asked.

'Yes, it's her. Well done!'

'She's an actress called Marion Underhill. Nothing spectacular, small parts in rep and so on.'

'How did you strike lucky so soon?'

'It wasn't just luck. You helped. An actress with horticultural experience, you said. On the off-chance I ran blonde gardening actresses through the Home Office computer. Much to my surprise, out she came.'

'But why did she become a computer entry?'

'Three years for malicious damage and arson, committed on behalf of the animal liberation movement. She did most of her sentence in an open prison where there's a big nursery garden to keep them happy and out of mischief.'

'So that's where she got her horticultural experience?'

'Yes, but as occupational therapy it hasn't exactly succeeded. It's only switched her from violence in defence of animals to violence in defence of plants.'

'D'you mind if I pass this on to my head gardener, Bill Wilkins? I've kept everything you told me to myself, but you know the situation. I'm worried about him, he still needs an antidote to love.'

'Tell him the whole story, if you like. I gather he knows quite a lot of it already.'

'Thank you. You've no idea where Jenny is?'

'None at all. And we've had no luck in identifying the two men. From your description, the tall young one with the beard could be another member of the acting profession. We hope the Irishman is on the files in Belfast, he's the one who really worries us.'

'How about their car?'

'Bought second-hand at auction,' he said gloomily, 'by a man no one can provide a description of, who gave a false address.'

When she arrived at the nursery she gave Bill a summary of her dealings with Wilberforce, including her discovery of Jenny's criminal past. He said, 'OK, Celia,' and turned away.

'It's not OK,' she retorted. 'Bill, do try to snap out of it.'

'How can I? Women are a disaster, that's what.'

'Nonsense. The trouble is, you tend to choose disastrous women. Next time, bring whoever it is to me first and I'll tell you whether or not she's a sound proposition.'

As he glared at her angrily, Margaret Fortescue drove into the yard. She had come to collect the large herbaceous plants that Celia had ordered to fill the gaps left in her garden from the previous summer's drought. But she was driving a Porsche instead of her usual Range Rover, and its sporting design included no provision for transporting massive clumps of rheum and macleaya and crambe. 'Stupid of me, I'm sorry,' she commented when this was pointed out.

'Bill can bring them up this afternoon in the van,' said Celia.

'Oh, lovely. But Hodson's taking a few days off to attend a niece's wedding, so could he possibly plant them for me as well?'

It was a natural request. Bill often helped out in the Kenlake garden on jobs which were too big for Hodson to tackle on his own.

'OK, Mrs Fortescue. I'll be up there two-ish.'

'Oh dear, could you make it a bit later, say half-past

three? I've people to lunch and you know how they stay.'

Her tone was light, but something seemed to be going on. Her smile was inviting, but Bill was looking sullen. 'Very well, then,' he said rather sullenly. 'We'll make it half-past three.'

A pang of suspicion hit Celia. Margaret Fortescue must have known that there was no way of getting the plants she had ordered into a Porsche. Why had she not come in something less awkward? Obviously, to ensure that Bill would have to bring them to Kenlake in the van. But why half-past three and not two? Why could he not do the planting while she entertained guests to lunch?

Celia's mind went back to two occasions in the past few months when she and Bill had been working in the Kenlake garden, and Mrs Fortescue had unobtrusively found a reason for Bill to stay behind with her after Celia had left. And now here she was, insisting on him coming after her guests had gone. Why? Was she hoping to lure him into her bed? If that was it, no wonder he would have preferred to avoid a tête-à-tête with her. She was one of Archerscroft's best customers. If her behaviour became embarrassing, he could hardly afford to be rude.

'Mrs Fortescue isn't bothering you?' she asked.

'She's OK.' But he avoided her eyes and sounded uncomfortable.

Perhaps Margaret's mysterious night-time lover existed after all. For a moment she amused herself with the thought that it could be Wilfrid Edgeley. A dark-haired woman might easily fall for his vapid blond prettiness. An affair with her would be a neat way of punishing his termagant of a wife, who prided herself on being on visiting terms at Kenlake.

Bill spent the whole afternoon there and was not back at the nursery before it closed. Questioned in the morning, he volunteered that Mrs Fortescue had invited him in for a beer after he finished work.

'She's a nice woman,' said Celia. When he did not react, she added: 'You do get on with her all right?'

83

The sullen look came back for a moment. 'She's OK.'

Celia wondered what to make of this. When Bill said a woman was OK it meant that she showed no tendency to pester him sexually. But if Margaret Fortescue was OK in that sense, what was the meaning of the sullen look?

'Oh, she said would I give you a message,' Bill remembered. 'She says if you're in trouble over money for the Chelsea thing, you've only to ask her.'

This was startling. How did Margaret Fortescue know that this was a good moment to produce a reminder of her promise? Not from Bill. With so much else to tell him, she had not mentioned the contretemps with George Bond. The crisis with the Admiral had blown up only the night before. How had the grapevine functioned with such extraordinary speed? Through Wilfrid Edgeley during a midnight tryst?

Later that morning Mrs Cadogan rang her at the office to say that the Admiral had relented. 'He used some rather quarter-deck expressions to say what Mrs Fortescue could do with her money, and he was very cross with you. Did she really offer to pay up, or did you invent it to call his bluff?'

'Oh, the offer's quite genuine. She's rather amused about the whole thing.'

'But it looks as if her husband isn't. Men are such children, don't you think? Fortescue's quite impossible, and keeping George out of mischief is becoming a whole-time job.'

'I can't help being sorry for him,' said Celia. 'Is he very upset?'

'Oh, no, dear. He's had a new idea and he's very excited about it. You know those little cottages at the bottom end of the High Street that back on to Baker's Meadow? George has worked it out that Fortescue would have to buy several of them and knock them down to get access to the site, so that he could build on it. George is going to get them listed as historic buildings to stop him.'

'Goodness. Those cottages aren't exactly architectural gems.'

'No, and they're just outside the conservation area. But knocking them down would spoil the view up the street, so he may get a listing for them. Even if he doesn't, making out the application will keep him happy for a bit.'

Preparations for Chelsea were now in full swing. Passes had been ordered for the team which would spend six hectic days constructing the garden. After much thought, Celia had decided that though the Admiral would be a useless passenger on the site, and probably an infernal nuisance, it would be impossible to keep him at home. The team would therefore have to number five: herself, Bill, Fred Tunney, the Admiral, and James Carstairs to contribute the effort of which the Admiral was physically and temperamentally incapable. Wilfrid Edgeley had begged to be allowed to come, in order to get away from his wife, but she had rejected him as too ineffective to be any use.

A mock-up of the proposed layout had been put together in the Admiral's garage, with the dimensions carefully marked on the floor. There was to be a raised area at the back of the site with an arbour on it covered with climbing roses, and to save carting masses of earth and rubble to Chelsea to raise the level, a stout wooden dais had been constructed, heavy enough to support a largish expanse of York stone paving as well as the arbour. The paving had been cut to shape and the pieces numbered, so that they would be easy to arrange when they were relaid. Water for the pool and electricity to run the pump under the fountain had been requisitioned from the show manager and paid for. Container-grown climbing roses for the arbour had been ordered from a firm which specialized in forcing them into flower in May and hiring them out to exhibitors at Chelsea. As they had to stay in their containers and be returned intact after the show, holes had been made in the paving and the platform underneath it to house the containers and make it seem that they were growing in small beds.

One of the glasshouses at Archerscroft was full of

plants earmarked for Chelsea, white and pink azaleas, intermediate irises in various pastel shades, spiraeas, a small purple acer, pale blue camassias, and tulips in great numbers to satisfy the appetite of the judges who tended, when faced with a close contest, to award the prize to the garden containing the highest count of blooms. Like every other exhibitor in the weeks before the show, Celia was haunted by the fear that all this would come into bloom either too early or too late. But unlike most of the other exhibitors, she had a more serious worry. Perhaps if she concentrated on the job in hand, and tried to forget she had ever met Superintendent Wilberforce, she would succeed in fighting down her fear of a terrorist outrage at Chelsea by the Fighters of the Green Front.

Five

'So there it is, ladies and gentlemen,' said the President
of the Royal Horticultural Society. 'Before the meeting
decides how to handle this very unpleasant development,
I think you should hear for yourselves what Superintendent Wilberforce has to say.'

Wilberforce rose. The Society's Council, meeting in
emergency session at its headquarters in Vincent Square,
inspected his lugubrious face with its drooping eyes and
mouth, and were depressed by its severity. He looked
like the sort of dedicated policeman who lived in a flat
and never in his life cultivated so much as a pot plant:
not the sort of man whom a gathering of experts on
everything from succulent euphorbias to the layout of
Elizabethan knot gardens could relate to easily.

'Thank you, ladies and gentlemen,' he began. 'May I
start by asking you to treat everything I am about to tell
you as confidential, and to keep as quiet as possible about
the fact that this meeting has taken place. We are following up some promising lines of enquiry, and it is possible
that we shall get results before the show opens. Meanwhile, no useful purpose would be served by allowing the
media to become over-excited and cause a premature
panic among the public. Sooner or later they are bound
to discover what is going on. At that stage you will no
doubt think it necessary to make some public announcement, but we would like to avoid all publicity till the last
possible moment and hope you will keep in touch with
us about the timing of anything you decide to say.

'As you know, large numbers of leaflets threatening

violence in support of environmental causes have been distributed during the past week. It is regrettable that so far none of the people dumping large quantities of them on the floors of supermarkets, underground trains, and so on have been arrested, but the operation has been organized with considerable skill so that the distributor has time to make his getaway before the leaflets are discovered. The leaflets make no specific threat to disrupt the Chelsea Flower Show, but rumours about a threat of violence at the show are very widespread in environmental circles. There has obviously been a leak, but not, we think, by a disaffected member of the organization who has decided to betray their plans. If that is the explanation, why is he content to run around spreading rumours, instead of contacting the Royal Horticultural Society or the police? We think this is an "official" leak of the type favoured by politicians, in other words information released by an organization which wishes it to be known, but is not prepared to announce it attributably.

'The question we have to decide is whether we are dealing with a serious threat, or with a hoax mounted to secure publicity for green causes. It is of course possible that green-minded people exist who are mad enough to think that the public would consider it an eco-friendly gesture, likely to win them adherents, if they killed or maimed scores of gardening enthusiasts in a terrorist operation. One can't wholly exclude this possibility, but the evidence for assuming a hoax is fairly strong. I will explain our reasons for taking this view in a moment.

'Even if we were a hundred per cent certain that this is a hoax we would have to treat it seriously. That means maintaining tight security from the moment when exhibitors arrive and begin to mount their displays. You already have an admirable method of dealing with a bomb scare during the show. A modified version of this system might be used while the show is being prepared, but we think it impractical to search all the consignments of plants and so on as the exhibitors bring them in. You also have a watertight system of passes to prevent unauthorized persons from entering the site, and if the exhibitors search their stands regularly we should be reasonably secure. You only allocate stands to firms with a good track record as exhibitors at the monthly shows in Vincent Square, but a firm could be hi-jacked for terrorist purposes. So please keep your eyes open for any stand that isn't being manned by the usual people, especially if the exhibit isn't quite what you would expect from that firm. We shall of course have plain-clothes officers on the site during the run-up to the show, and during it. When it opens we shall also have enough men on the gates to search handbags and so on thoroughly.

'You all know as well as I do that despite all these precautions absolute security cannot be guaranteed. But there are good reasons for believing that we are dealing with a hoax. If we assume that this organization means what it says, and really intends to commit some outrage, why is it forfeiting the advantages of surprise? Why warn us, knowing that we will take stringent safety precautions to frustrate them? There is an obvious answer, which I would like you to consider. The security operation at Chelsea will inevitably attract the attention of the media almost at once. They will start asking questions which will have to be answered. The whole thing will become public knowledge well before the show opens. So why should they bother to let off so much as a stink-bomb? The furore of publicity will have made their propaganda point for them already. Failure to make good their threat of violence will be a plus, not a minus. They will have hurt no one, and a section of the public will be delighted by the way they have cocked a snook at the horticultural establishment, the police, and the media, and made us all look ridiculous. Terrorism is theatre, drama aimed at an audience. In this case the audience is being entertained at the terrorist theatre of the absurd.

'These, briefly, are our reasons for advising you that we think we are dealing with a hoax, though a very ingenious one. At the same time, we cannot be entirely certain of this, and shall have to do what we do in all such doubtful cases, and take security precautions on the assumption that the threat is real.

'That is all I can tell you at this stage. As the enquiry proceeds, we will keep you informed.'

'Thank you, Superintendent,' said the President as Wilberforce sat down. 'Before we proceed further, are there any questions? Yes, Professor.'

The professor, a world authority on genetically engineered viruses, seemed to be addressing himself to the ceiling. 'Is there any evidence that this organization actually exists? If all we have is some leaflets and a mass of rumour, passed from mouth to mouth in a section of the public which enjoys frightening itself with doomsday predictions, perhaps we need not take the matter too seriously.'

'Caches of IRA-type detonators and rifle ammunition have been found,' Wilberforce replied. 'Clearly, the organization exists, but we have evidence that it is trying to make us believe that it is larger and perhaps more violent than is actually the case.'

After a few more questions, the President thanked him and said: 'Now, before we debate ways and means, there is one question to be got out of the way. I take it that no one here is in favour of giving in to these people and cancelling the show?'

Back at the Yard, Wilberforce told his team of detectives what had happened. 'One or two of them shifted in their chairs and looked queasy, but the old gentleman was standing no nonsense and shamed them all into standing firm. Then they had quite a sensible general discussion, but the RHS Council is a bit too grand to deal with the nuts and bolts of a thing like this, so I had a separate meeting with their Show Manager and his staff to tie up details. That went well too, but there's one snag. They've packed the show ground so tight that there's nowhere for them to put an incident room for us. We'll be in the ordinary police tent.'

'What? Along with the pickpockets and the old ladies

who've lost their umbrellas?' protested Inspector Grigg, his second-in-command.

'We'll try to organize a van alongside and off-load all that into it. I'll tell you what really worries me though. Our chances of keeping the lid on the publicity for more than a day or two are pretty dim. The opposition will want the longest run-up of panic they can manage, and if they don't get in first with a warning, people who've heard the rumours will start unburdening themselves to the media, and a lot of old women of both sexes will suddenly decide that they hate flower shows anyway.'

'Unless we crack the thing open first,' said Grigg.

His team was making strenuous efforts to do so. Monica Porter's background was being investigated. The country pub near Melbury where the two men in the BMW had stayed had been identified, but a forwarding address found there by the detectives proved to be the first clue in a treasure-hunt trail leading to Keeper's Cottage.

'An extra precaution,' Wilberforce commented, 'in case Mrs Grant wasn't quick enough on the uptake.'

Their white BMW was on a nation-wide wanted list, but had been bought at a second-hand-car auction by a man calling himself Smith, who gave a false address and did not correspond to the description of either of them. If the blue-chinned Irishman had an IRA background, there was a hope that Army Intelligence in Northern Ireland would have some record of him. A faxed enquiry to them had drawn a blank, but Inspector Grigg was about to leave for Belfast and make more detailed enquiries in person.

Meanwhile Wilberforce and Sergeant Padstow set off up the motorway to question the Tidmarshes at the organic commune near Birmingham where they were in conference. On arriving, they found that it gave the lie to the popular fancy that a commune is disorderly by definition, and that 'organic' means that the crops will be pest-ridden. Wilberforce was struck by its air of business-like prosperity. The fields and vegetable plots were neatly cultivated. There was a crowd of buyers round the stall from which its produce was sold. Offices and living quarters for the commune's inmates were provided in a Victorian mansion of forbidding ugliness, which was not, however, in a state of mock-Gothic disrepair.

They explained who they were and what they wanted to a group of people standing near the front door. The atmosphere became icy. Nobody actually called them 'pigs', but clearly that was what they were.

'You'd better go inside and talk to Martin,' said someone in a voice of carefully calculated boredom.

Martin, seated in his office, was a youngish man whose resolute air and firm chin probably accounted for the establishment's air of prosperity and order. He sent for the Tidmarshes and was soon joined by Wendy, an ample woman in a very ethnic blouse, and her weedy husband in becomingly ragged jeans.

'You can talk to them in here,' Martin conceded.

Wilberforce thanked him and waited for him to go.

'I want to know what you're asking them about,' said Martin, standing his ground.

'Mr and Mrs Tidmarsh can tell you that afterwards if they wish,' replied Wilberforce, and went on waiting patiently.

Martin went, with very bad grace. The Tidmarshes looked after him anxiously, as if his departure removed their last line of defence against police brutality. When Sergeant Padstow opened his notebook, they shuddered.

'I have only a few very simple questions,' Wilberforce began, 'about these rumours concerning the Chelsea Flower Show.'

'Rumours?' Wendy asked, raising her eyebrows.

'Surely you must have heard them? Rumours to the effect that environmental extremists plan to commit a terrorist outrage at the show?'

Edward's Adam's apple rose and fell.

'No, I don't think so,' said Wendy. 'Are there really stories about this going round, or are your paid informers overworking their imaginations?'

'The rumours are very widespread. I find it difficult to believe that you haven't heard them, moving as you do in environment-conscious circles, and holding the views that you do.'

'How does he know what views I hold?' Wendy asked of no one in particular.

'You make no secret of them in your neighbourhood at home.'

She flew into a sudden panic. 'So you've been snooping around there, have you. Why are you investigating us? What are you accusing us of?'

'Nothing, but there's a connection between these rumours and your home village of Melbury.'

'So you suspect us? Why us? Just because we support green causes and practise alternative horticulture? Oh, really, this is the sort of thing that gives the police a bad name.'

'I'm not accusing you of anything, and I'm not "investigating" you. But I believe you attend conferences about environmental issues from time to time?'

'There's nothing wrong in that, is there?' squeaked Edward.

'Not that I'm aware of. But there's a connection between the rumours and your neighbour Mrs Grant, who—'

'Oh, really, Superintendent, only a policeman could be stupid enough to suspect Celia Grant. She's much too much of a lady to go in for terrorism.'

Wilberforce paused ominously. 'Sergeant, which of us is stupid? Me, or a woman who interrupts what I'm trying to tell her with the silliest remark I've heard in a month of Sundays?'

'Well, Super,' rumbled Padstow, 'I reckon that if the lady just listened to your questions and answered them, it would save everyone's time.'

'Shall we stop playing games now,' said Wilberforce severely. 'This is a serious matter, with the lives of innocent people at stake.'

Wendy suddenly sobered up. 'I'm sorry, Superintendent, it was silly of me to play games. Of course I've heard the rumours, I'm as worried about them as you are. Do please put your questions.'

'Thank you. Our concern is that Mrs Grant seems to have been targeted by these people as the victim of an elaborate deception plan. Someone must have drawn their attention to her.'

She considered this calmly. 'And because we're her neighbours you think it could have been us?'

'It's a possibility that I have to look into.'

'So you want us to tell you whether we're terrorists or not.'

'Yes, please.'

'Well, we aren't.'

'Thank you. My next question is whether either of you recall mentioning Mrs Grant to any of your contacts in the movement, perhaps at a conference, or being questioned by anyone about her. We're specially interested to know how they found out that she had a reputation as an amateur detective.'

Edward's Adam's apple began working overtime. Wendy seemed to be searching her memory. 'I see what you mean, but I don't recall mentioning her to anyone, do you Edward?'

'No,' said Edward. 'Environmental conferences are about serious issues, there's not much time for gossip.'

'So I'm sorry, I'm afraid we can't help you,' said Wendy with a winning smile.

Wilberforce went on probing for a time. What conferences had they attended? Had anyone with an Irish accent been there? The Tidmarshes were sympathetic, but unable to help. Wilberforce was in two minds. Should he, or should he not put the boot in? He was far from sure that they were telling the truth, and as Mrs Grant's neighbours they were the obvious suspects. He would be justified in holding them for questioning under the Prevention of Terrorism Act and trying to batter a confession out of them. On the other hand they had behaved quite reasonably when they realized that they weren't being accused

94

of anything. Mrs Grant might be right, they stood out so obviously as suspects that they could well be innocent. Even if they were not, there were good tactical reasons for giving them the benefit of the doubt for the moment. If the commune proved on investigation to be a terrorist nerve centre, nothing would have been gained by putting on the frighteners too soon and raising the alarm. So he told the Tidmarshes how to get in touch with him if they remembered anything significant, and brought the interview to an end.

'What d'you reckon, Super?' Padstow asked as they drove away. 'Were they holding out on us?'

'I'm not sure. If she was putting on an act it was quite a good one.'

'He was looking pretty seasick, though.'

'Perhaps he's simply the nervous type. I decided to let it go. If that commune turns out to be a terrorist hotbed we'll pull them in when we're ready. Let's find out if the locals know anything about the place.'

But the commune's reputation with the local police turned out to be orderly and law abiding.

'If we get something to throw at them, we can go back. That secretary of Mrs Grant's may give us a lead.'

Back in London, he found an envelope waiting for him on his desk. It had been posted in central London, and contained a leaflet like the ones found at Keeper's Cottage. With it was a typewritten note: 'Special Branch take notice. Communications from the Fighters of the Green Front will be authenticated with the codeword St Finians. Other messages can be dismissed as hoaxes. P.S. Anyone who thinks we are hoaxers is in for a rude shock.'

The name had an Irish flavour. Wilberforce checked with Army Intelligence in Belfast. Four years ago, 'St Finians' had been used as an authenticating codeword by the IRA.

For some days the media had been in an excited state about the leaflets threatening violence against firms dealing in peat and horticultural chemicals, many of which had been left lying about in public places. Now a new

95

twist was given to the story by a report in one of the papers about 'rumours which are rife in the innermost circles of the green movement'. It was headed 'Eco-terrorism at the Chelsea Flower Show?' but the question mark did little to cast doubt on the alarming import of what followed. In no time at all the Director General of the RHS was on the line. Should they not put out a press release at once, to the effect that the alleged threat was believed by the police to be a hoax?

Wilberforce was against this. 'If we say it's a hoax, we force them to retort publicly that it's nothing of the kind, and that anyone who dares to set foot in the show is making himself a legitimate target and will be massacred.' Instead, they told the media that the police were aware of the rumours, and were investigating.

Next day, no newspaper was complete without a dozen column inches about the 'Chelsea eco-terror'. Experts on green issues had a field day, including some who maintained that if their warnings against pollution by danger-ous chemicals were not heeded, the campaign for the defence of the environment would inevitably take on a violent form. Wilberforce waited gloomily for the moment when the media began to ask: 'What are the police doing? The public have a right to know.'

Celia was horrified by the press furore and the damage it was doing to her beloved RHS. She could imagine what its officers must be going through, but was determined not to let herself be involved in their agonizing deliber-ations. Her contact with the investigation had been inci-dental, she decided. She had provided information to the police, nothing more.

A week of press-induced panic later, it was still dark when she set off for Chelsea in the Archerscroft van with Bill, Fred Tunney, and James Carstairs to do the heavy work. Parking on the site was at a premium, and it was essential to be there when it opened at six, to secure a place where the first consignment of raw materials for the courtyard garden could be off-loaded.

Wilberforce had asked her to keep in touch with him when she arrived at Chelsea, and in due course she presented herself at his incident room, but only to impress on him that she wanted to stay right out of the picture. She was still determined to keep very quiet about her minor involvement in the eco-terror enquiry. It was not just a matter of avoiding notoriety. By isolating herself from the whole thing, and going about her business at the show as if nothing unusual was happening, she would also be able to preserve an uneasy peace of mind.

Over the next few days of hard work the little garden took shape. The Admiral, who was staying at his West End club, looked in from time to time to get in everyone's way and make fatuous suggestions. There were the inevitable panics: when the containers for the climbing roses on the arbour proved too large for the holes made for them; when the electricity supply for the fountain in the pool failed to materialize; when the purple acer in the far corner threatened to overhang the exhibit in the neighbouring courtyard, a dreadful violation of the rules. At intervals a loudspeaker message summoned Mr Farquharson to the telephone. This was a coded signal asking all exhibitors to search their stands for explosives. Celia did so conscientiously, but her rigid control of her nerves suffered in the process.

Sergeant John Hodges of the Dorset police was a man of old-fashioned ideas, who would have liked to put the clock back to the days when a policeman's patch was the village where he lived. In those days he had been a respected member of the community who knew everyone's business and moved about on foot, or for longer distances on a bicycle. He still lived in the village, a collection of thatched cottages strung out along one of the chalk streams which flow into the River Stour. But the Dorset force had moved with the times, and he now had to work over a much wider area from a squad car based in the nearest town. He hated being caged in it without a proper patch of his own, and did his best to keep in touch with the affairs of the village in his spare time, having a quiet word with turbulent youngsters before they fell foul of the law, and keeping an eye on any potential trouble spots.

One of the places that aroused suspicious queries in his mind was Townley's Trout Farm, a few miles downstream from the village. It had gone bankrupt two years ago, after the fish caught a disease and the owner suffered a heart attack. Back in the summer it had been sold to a firm which had erected a high wire fence round it and fitted a padlock on the equally high gate. But there were no obvious signs of activity within, let alone any attempt to sell trout. The faded signboard at the entrance still described the place as Townley's Trout Farm, but a sticker pasted over it added the information 'closed'. No one seemed to be living in the cottage attached to the farm.

Desultory comings and goings suggested that something was going on there. A young man in a Ford Fiesta who had been seen letting himself in through the padlocked gate volunteered later to a fascinated lunchtime audience in the village pub that the place was being used as a centre for research into diseases affecting farmed fish. In view of the previous history of disease there, this seemed plausible, and the young man's claim to be a scientific researcher was corroborated by the white linen coat on view in the back of his car.

But the research seemed to be very intermittent, involving a visit once or twice a week by the young man in the Ford Fiesta. On one occasion he had been accompanied by a blonde young woman whose alluring appearance, tight-fitting jeans, and blasphemous language during the lunchtime session at the pub had prompted hours of lascivious speculation among the regulars. But nothing else had happened to attract Sergeant Hodges' interest till a week ago, when a sudden burst of activity had broken out. A road mender clearing the ditches near by told him that a party of men on powerful motorcycles had arrived and installed themselves in the empty cottage.

Next day when he drove past himself a covered truck was parked in front of the office building, and the men were loading something into it, but the way the truck was positioned prevented him from seeing what the load was.

The motorcycles worried him a little, but he saw no reason to suspect anything illegal. Presumably the research programme had been completed and stores were being removed. But when he drove past on his way to work on the following day, there was a change. The motorcyclists and the truck had gone. The gates were open, and a car was standing in front of the office building. He drove in. The office door was open. He looked in, then withdrew quickly. Inside, a small dark man with a very blue shave was locked in a full frontal embrace with a blonde, presumably the one whose appearance in the pub had caused such a sensation.

Hodges coughed, allowed time for any necessary adjustment of clothing and walked in to find the dark man packing items of stationery from the desk drawers into an attaché case. The blonde, leaning casually against the wall, treated Hodges to a bold stare which confirmed him in his view that she was a shameless hussy.

Ignoring her, he addressed himself to the dark man. 'Good afternoon, sir. I hope you don't mind my asking, but is the research programme here finished?'

'Yes, we wound it up two days ago, I'm just making sure nothing's been left behind. You're the local bobby, are you?'

'That's right, sir. Will you be selling the place?'

'Oh, it doesn't belong to me. I'm just the project director for the research.'

'Then perhaps you'd be good enough to tell me who the owner is, so that we can get in touch in case of vandalism and so on.'

'I can't tell you offhand. Give me your address and I'll find out and let you know.'

Hodges gave him the details. As he left he noticed the car for the first time. It was a white two-door BMW with damage to the offside front wing. A tiny doubt sprang up in his mind. There was an entry among the Wanteds for a BMW with a damaged wing.

At the station he looked up the details. It was the offside front wing that was damaged on the wanted car. The registration number did not correspond, but that could have been changed. The driver was described as small and dark, with a blue shave. His identikit picture resembled the man Hodges had seen at the trout farm, but he had spoken posh English, with no trace of the Irish accent which the wanted man was supposed to have.

Two other people were wanted in connection with the case, a tall bearded man and a blonde woman called Marion Underhill, an actress whose glamorous features and blonde curls figured in the police records in a copy of a carefully posed and lit studio portrait. But she had a prison record; there was also a mug shot of her, looking sulky in an Afro hair-do. Hodges thought he could see a resemblance between her and the bold-faced blonde at the trout farm. Despite the wrong registration number and the driver's lack of an Irish accent, he decided to play safe and make a report.

He was not prepared for the speed of the reaction. Next morning he was called back urgently to headquarters from the scene of a burglary to be questioned in great detail about his discovery by two men from the Special Branch in London. When he had described his observations in great detail, they let him go back on patrol.

'How about it, Jim?' said Inspector Grigg to his teammate John Foster. 'The motorcyclists are right, and there were some in the report about that cottage near Amesbury. Amesbury's not that far from here.'

'There's one thing wrong, though. No Irish accent.'

'Perhaps he can disguise it when he wants to. Anyway, we better look.'

The padlock in the formidable gate of the Townley Trout Farm presented no real difficulty. Grigg opened up and Foster drove into the yard.

The office building was locked. Only a dilapidated desk and a chair were visible through the window.

'Hodges says the chap cleaned everything out,' said Foster. 'Better break in and make sure, though.'

They picked the lock. The interior yielded only a few paper clips, spilled in the corner of the drawer, so they turned their attention to the installation outside.

Never having been in a trout farm before, they studied it with interest. Grigg, who had done some coarse fishing, remembered that trout needed running water to survive, and he soon worked out how the thing functioned. The long concrete troughs for the fish ran parallel to each other across a gentle slope. Water flowed into each trough from the one above through a pipe at one end, and delivered it to the trough below through a similar pipe at the other end. The result when the apparatus was working was a fast-flowing waterfall through the concrete troughs from top to bottom, with trout swimming against the current at every level. But there were no trout now, and the water was still.

'Where did the water supply come from?' Foster asked. 'There's no stream.'

Under a wooden casing they discovered the pump which recycled the contents of the bottom trough back to the top.

'It could have been them here,' Grigg decided after they had searched the place thoroughly. 'But there's nothing left here now. Back to HQ, eh?'

On the way back to the car, Grigg stopped in his tracks and slapped the back of his neck hard. 'Strewth! Something's stung me.'

'It bloody has,' said Foster. 'You got blood all over your collar.'

Cooped up in the undersized, overcrowded incident room, Wilberforce decided he must escape for a few minutes or go mad. The inconclusive result of Grigg's excursion to Dorset had not provided the breakthrough he needed so badly. Only forty-eight hours remained before the show opened to the RHS membership on Tuesday. Everything now was staked on the hope that the whole thing was a hoax. A high-level RHS delegation told him that the media pressure for a statement could no longer be resisted. Together they concocted a press release: the police were taking every precaution possible against a terrorist attack at the show, and as they had been warned in advance they were confident that their precautions would be effective. It was most unusual for terrorists to announce their target to the authorities in advance, and there were strong reasons for suspecting a publicity stunt in favour of green causes by persons who had no intention of endangering life.

Predictably, this provoked an immediate reply, widely published next day in the media:

THE ORGANIZERS OF THE OBSCENE POISON EXHIBITION AT CHELSEA

So far you have been prevented from cancelling the show by pressure from the commercial interests which are your paymasters. They rely for their profits on selling environmentally dangerous chemicals to the gardening public, and on ruining Sites of Special Scientific Interest by the ruthless extraction of peat. The show is a legitimate target because of your subservience to such people. You are urgently advised to reconsider your position.

The suggestion that we are engaged in a harmless publicity stunt is an insult for which you will pay dearly. You are to ensure that everyone is out of the show ground by 8 a.m. on Tuesday, and that it remains empty till it is scheduled to close on Friday. Should you fail to do so, you, not us, will be responsible for the very serious consequences.

The Fighters of the Green Front

In spite of this challenge the RHS stood firm: the show would go on. But Wilberforce was not the only one to have visions of blood flowing among the banks of flowers.

Wandering through the show ground while the exhibitors put the final touches to their stands, he faced up grimly to the uncertainties of the battle ahead. But unlike

102

Shakespeare's Henry V, wandering in disguise through the English camp on the eve of Agincourt, he could not draw reassurance from the conversation of the common soldiers. The soldiery of the Chelsea Flower Show was far too busy, and must not be asked to share his alarm.

The episode at the trout farm nagged at his mind. He felt guiltily that it was trying to tell him something. But what?

Half-way along the main avenue he came on an area divided by low brick walls into a series of small courtyards. The end one, nearest the avenue, contained a charming composition in pastel shades, with a rose-covered arbour at the back and a pool set in the grass with a lead figurine in the middle of it. A woman, bent double over one of the beds, was planting white azaleas. She straightened and he recognized Mrs Grant.

She turned, caught his eye and looked away. He remembered that she was anxious not to get involved in his problems and was about to move away. But on a sudden impulse he beckoned to her, then moved on a few yards down the avenue, away from her fellow workers in the courtyard garden. With a nervous glance over her shoulder, she followed.

'Mrs Grant, have you any ideas about this? What could the Green Front have been getting up to at a trout farm?'

'I can't imagine, Superintendent. Why d'you ask?'

He told her the circumstances. 'We've no proof that it was them, but we think so. I've been cudgelling my brains about it all morning. Why a trout farm?'

'I've no idea. Where is it?'

'In Dorset, somewhere near Blandford. If anything occurs to you, do give me a ring, won't you?'

Any thoughts she might have had about trout farms were chased out of her mind by the sight of Admiral Bond, standing in the middle of the avenue and staring after Wilberforce.

'Who was that?' he asked her.

'A man from one of the rose firms in Norfolk,' she lied. 'But I forget his name.'

Wilberforce strolled on. In the big marquee he came

face to face with Peter Walton, his opposite number from the Anti-Terrorist Squad at the Yard. The division of responsibilities between them was clear, though not necessarily logical. He was responsible to MI5 for gathering intelligence about projected terrorist activities and if possible ensuring that they did not occur. When they had occurred, Walton arrived on the scene and took over the search for fragments of the detonator, the arrest of suspects, and the assembly of a prosecution case.

'Thought I'd have a look-see, on the off-chance,' Walton explained.

Wilberforce managed a smile. Walton was within his rights, of course. But by making a visit of inspection before the event he was behaving rather like a vulture, hovering before the corpse was dead.

By three o'clock, Melbury Garden Society's courtyard garden was as near to a state of grace as it ever would be. It only remained for Celia to prevent the others from ruining the effect by further attempts to titivate it. This she managed by inviting them to tea at her club off Sloane Street and delaying them there till it was too late to return. After the strain of commuting from Melbury in the small hours for a week, she had decided to spend the last two nights at the club, and settled down to what ought to have been a restful evening. But the tensions and fears had followed her from the show ground. She was far from convinced that the terrorist threat was a hoax. Logic suggested that it was, but there was no shortage in the world of people whose pent-up fury left no room for logic. Over her lonely evening meal in the club's dining room she brooded on visions of disaster.

Another uncomfortable vision kept cropping up unbidden into her mind, of herself fishing a trout pool in the upper reaches of the Stour in Dorset. Her Uncle Hugo had been with her. She had enjoyed it at the time. Why was the memory of it uncomfortable now? Not just uncomfortable. It filled her with a vague dread.

Dismissing these gloomy thoughts as far as possible,

she went to bed and presently suffered from her standard nightmare, to the effect that she was a pot-bound saxifrage. Her roots were suffering cruelly from their confinement in the pot, but the Admiral was refusing to pot her on because, according to him, there was no room for a larger pot in the Chelsea layout. Then came a terrifying explosion. Liberated from her pot, she had become human again. But all around her, among the shattered flowers of Chelsea, people were dying.

She woke with a start, shook off the horror, and took stock. Presently she realized that her subconscious, besides giving her a nightmare, had been busy with something less alarming, and was now serving it up by way of compensation for her distress. It was arranging her memory of the trout pool five miles above Blandford alongside Wilberforce's mention of a trout farm and coupling them with something Uncle Hugo had said. With a stir of interest, she realized that in combination they might mean something.

It was more than a stir now. A suspicion, perhaps even a brilliant flash of inspiration. As an answer to the security problem at Chelsea, it belonged in the realms of fantasy. But it had a sort of insane logic. Brooding over it in the small hours, she decided that there was probably nothing in it, but it must be checked.

As soon as it was decent to ring a distinguished ex-ambassador in his seventies she did so, and made him repeat in more detail what he had told her in outline as they fished side by side. Encouraged to think that there might be something in her idea, she asked him: 'Who's the authority on this?'

'A laboratory of some kind in Wareham. I think it's called the Freshwater Research Establishment. What's all this about, Celia? Has someone committed a very recherché crime?'

'Sorry, Uncle Hugo, I can't talk now, have to tell you later. Be an angel and look up this place in your phone book, would you?'

Supplied with the number, she rang it and raised what

105

sounded like the night watchman. With the aid of some brisk bullying she extracted from him the home number of the scientist in charge. Her conversation with him, conducted in mounting excitement, lasted for almost half an hour. When it was over she rang Wilberforce's incident room at Chelsea and asked to speak to him urgently.

There was a delay while he was fetched back from examining a late exhibit of bromeliads whose packing material was regarded as suspect. 'Tell me,' she began without preamble, 'did any of the policemen who went to that trout farm get bitten by an insect?'

'Yes. One of them did. Why?'

'Quite a vicious bite, like a horsefly's?'

'Yes.'

'Good.'

'No, Mrs Grant, not good. It's swollen up and gone septic. He's quite a sight.'

'I'm sorry about that, but it confirms that I'm right. I've got the answer to your conundrum. I know what's going to happen at Chelsea.'

'Tell me.'

'You can stop looking for Semtex among the pot plants, that's not on the agenda. The show's going to be attacked with a terror weapon you've probably never heard of, because so far it's only operated in a small area of Dorset. It's known as the Blandford fly.'

Six

'Was that what stung John Grigg?' Wilberforce asked.

'Yes, they must have been breeding them at the trout farm. The idea is to punish everyone who visits this eco-hostile show by tormenting them with insect bites that go septic.'

'Hell,' said Wilberforce, thinking how little time he had left to counter the threat. There was only the rest of the day, which was earmarked for judging the exhibits and the press show, and in the afternoon a private view for the Queen and assorted members of the royal family. At eight next morning the show would be opened to the vast membership of the RHS, and at the same moment the attack by the Green Front would begin.

'You're sure this is really practical?' he asked Celia.

'Yes. I've been talking to the expert on the Blandford fly at a laboratory in Wareham. Look, I'm at my club, fifteen minutes away. Why don't you phone Wareham and tell them your fax number, they've got together some background material to send to you. I'll be with you by the time their material arrives.'

When she reached the incident room Wilberforce, Grigg and Foster were poring over a faxed reprint of an article in the *Journal of Applied Ecology* entitled: 'Distribution of Oviposition Sites and Characteristics of Egg Development in the "Blandford fly" *Simulium posticatum*.'

'I suppose,' said Wilberforce, 'that an oviposition site is where you lay your eggs. This isn't going to be easy reading.'

107

'Would you like a quick run-down?' asked Celia, joining them. 'I had a long talk with the expert when I rang him.'

'Please,' he said with relief.

'He says the eggs are laid in summer, along the river bank above and below the weir at Blandford, but well above the summer waterline. Then they diapause till February—'

'Diapause?' he queried.

'They lie there dormant for six months. Plenty of time for you to collect eggs from the river bank and transfer them to your breeding station at the trout farm.'

'One moment, Mrs Grant,' Wilberforce interrupted. 'Where's Inspector Grigg? Oh, there you are. When did the local man notice signs of occupation at the trout farm?'

Grigg consulted his notebook. 'July last year, Super.'

'Good, that fits. Go on, Mrs Grant.'

'The start of the cold weather triggers the eggs off to start developing, and in February they hatch. The larvae find their way into the river, which is easy because the water level is higher than during the winter months. They then attach themselves to weed and so on and start feeding on algae and detritus which floats down the river. And this is the point. The larvae are quite unable to survive in still or slow-moving water. They'd die in a pond. But the conditions they like can be created artificially in a place where a rapid flow of water can be maintained, such as a trout farm.'

'Fine, but where do you get the algae and detritus for them to feed on?' asked Wilberforce.

'You don't. My expert says they're perfectly happy to gorge themselves on yeast. They go on doing that till early May, when they start to pupate. The pupae don't feed, they just lie on the bottom doing nothing. So it's perfectly easy to scoop them up out of the water at the trout farm, take them to Chelsea, and wait for them to hatch.'

'Mrs Grant, you are a marvel, and the RHS ought to

108

give you a medal the size of a dinner plate.' He frowned. 'But we've got to find these larvae and destroy them before they hatch. What do they look like?'

'He said you'd find a detailed description in the material he sent you.'

Wilberforce picked up the thickly typed sheets, interspersed with graphs and statistical tables, and groaned.

'There's something else he said he'd send, Superintendent. A paper written for lay people, to explain things to the suffering population of Blandford. I think this must be it.'*

He glanced through it. 'Here we are. "The pupae have a simple conical shape and, at the thick (front) end gill filaments project from the open mouth of the bivi. The pupae do not feed and, as they develop, their colour gradually darkens. After a few days the skin splits and the adult fly emerges within a bubble of air. The tiny air bubble rushes to the surface of the water and, as it bursts, the fly takes to the air." Hell, does that mean the pupae have to be in water?'

'Apparently, yes,' said Celia.

Wilberforce groaned, thinking of all the vases and other containers of water that would have to be emptied and searched, then studied the next paragraph of the document. 'Hey everyone, listen to this, it's a frightful scenario,' he said and began reading aloud.

' "The male flies collect in swarms which position themselves near prominent objects such as trees or the corner of buildings, awaiting the arrival of females. Mating pairs fall to the ground. Before or after mating the female flies frequently to seek a blood-meal to supplement their diet as the eggs are produced. The main host is man.

' "It is the blood-sucking habit of the Blandford fly which causes the major problem to residents of the district. In May and June female flies range far and wide in search of hosts. Most of the victims are bitten on the legs and the saliva of the fly, which passes into the wound,

* *The Blandford Fly*, by M. Ladle, Ph.D., Institute of Freshwater Ecology, Wareham, Dorset.

often causes severe irritation, pain, swelling, and blistering of the tissues. To reduce the chance of being bitten it is a good idea to wear trousers, to use insect repellant, and to avoid open areas in the middle of the day (biting activity is least in the early morning and late evening)." '

He put the paper down. 'How do we know the pupae won't start hatching out before eight tomorrow? Do we phone the Queen and tell her to smother herself in insect repellant and come in trousers and a headscarf this afternoon?'

A gloomy silence fell.

'Come on, then, let's get down to it,' he said wearily. 'This time calling Mr Farquharson means that they're all to search every drop of water in the place, not just the ornamental pools in the show gardens and the stands where they're exhibiting water lilies and such, but the vases with flowers in them as well.'

'No,' said Celia. 'The pupae aren't here yet.'

'They must be. If anything had to be smuggled in it's happened already. The exhibits are all set up. There's nothing more coming in.'

'No,' Celia repeated, 'they can't be. Some of the flies were out two days ago, look at poor Inspector Grigg's neck. If the pupae were in water here already, they'd be hatching out and some of us would have been bitten.'

Wilberforce nodded. 'Then how about a closed container? The flies hatch out in it and when the place is good and crowded the container's opened to let them out?'

'Who opens it?' asked Foster. 'Someone who melts away into the crowd?'

'Or gets lynched by it. Risky,' said Grigg. 'Something with a timing device, that opens of its own accord?'

'I'm trying to visualize this container,' Wilberforce murmured. 'It has to be biggish to be of any use. What sort of big container with a timing device is there on one of the stands that hasn't been spotted?'

'I don't think it has to be on a stand,' said Celia thoughtfully. 'They could open it outside the ground.'

Everyone looked at her.

'Imagine the situation inside this container. A lot of the flies have hatched out. Tomorrow, when the ground is full, you open the container in one of the neighbouring streets, and they fly out. They've been mating like mad in the confined space and the females are dying for a blood-meal. They're prepared to range far and wide if necessary. But what they see on the far side of the hedge isn't a meal, it's a Lord Mayor's Banquet.'

'Well done, Mrs Grant,' said Wilberforce quietly. 'Now let's start thinking all over again.'

'A car,' Grigg suggested. 'You stop for a moment in the Chelsea Bridge Road and you open the boot.'

'And the police close the boot and arrest you before half the flies are out,' Wilberforce objected.

'A van would be better,' said Foster, 'delivering something to one of the houses.'

'Same objection. One moment, though. The container could be – yes, it could be in a flat in one of the houses across the road. Or rather, the flat *is* the container. You put the pupae in the bath, and give the flies the run of the place. When the right moment comes, you open the front windows, and hey presto.'

Everyone thought about this new panorama of possibilities.

'Let's have another look at that residents' search list,' said Wilberforce.

Every house in the streets overlooking the show ground had been visited, and the bona fides of the occupants verified. Owners who had rented out their homes for the week for firms or individuals with business at the show were made to give details of their tenants, and a special watch was being kept on flats whose owners were away.

'So we run another check on the whole lot,' Wilberforce ordered. 'And damn quick too. Mrs Grant, you've been brilliant. I can't thank you enough. Without you, we'd still be sniffing around for Semtex. You've saved us.'

'Don't speak too soon. I'll leave you now to get on

111

with it. But you will make quite sure my name isn't leaked to the media in connection with all this?'

He looked at her doubtfully. 'You don't mean that?'

'Oh, I do,' she insisted. 'Please. I would hate it.'

'And I would hate taking credit for someone else's brilliant feat of deduction.'

'It will make up for when you do something clever you can't talk about, Superintendent. I must go now. I'm supposed to be sitting in judgement on flowering shrubs.'

As a member of Floral Committee B she had to join a panel of judges which scrutinized plants claimed by their breeders to be new and exceptionally meritorious, and give them an Award of Merit unless they seemed to be without exceptional merit, or not new. Her duties in the Plants for Award marquee kept her busy for most of the morning. For some arcane RHS reason the shrub committee also judged lilies, and as she peered into the throat of an unpleasant brick-red one with cyclamen-pink blotches and black stamens, she found herself wondering what Wilberforce and his men were doing, and what success they were having in their search. By the time she left the marquee to take her seat at the President's lunch, she had got herself into a fine old state of nerves, convinced that her allegedly brilliant feat of deduction was an appalling error of judgement; and that thanks to her stupidity, a great many policemen were laboriously tramping along a false trail.

The atmosphere at the lunch was far less carefree than usual. To keep the occasion civilized, the high priests of the horticultural world were discussing every subject except the one they were all thinking about. Towards the end of the meal this became effortful. One of Celia's neighbours defied the taboo and uttered the word 'hoax'. A lively discussion broke out. Wild theories were canvassed and a man opposite her announced, on the strength of something he had been told on the best authority at his club, that there was no question of it being anything but a hoax and a devious publicity stunt, mounted by a consortium of firms promoting various

112

substitutes for peat. Celia said nothing, and wondered if the search of premises overlooking the show ground was having any success.

In the afternoon the show, emptied of everyone but the exhibitors and a few cameramen, was on parade for the royal party. The exhibitors worried about positioning themselves so that the name of the firm would be in shot as they were filmed in conversation with royalty. The organizers, unconvinced that the invasion would not begin till next morning, clutched hastily purchased bottles of insect repellant in case it had to be applied to the monarch, and scanned the sky for signs that the attack had begun. The Queen showed no anxiety, though she had been warned. A threat of insect bites was as nothing after years of exposure to the danger of assassination.

The Admiral was in ecstasies. Melbury Garden Society's entry had won a silver medal. The fact that only two of the eight courtyard gardens had failed to win an award did nothing to damp down his sense of triumph. Only one exhibitor was allowed to man each stand during the visit of the royal party. This honour naturally fell to him, and he almost fell over himself with pride as he was graciously congratulated.

Wilberforce, meanwhile, was having his troubles. In response to an urgent summons the expert from Wareham had arrived to give advice, bringing with him spraying equipment to exterminate the flies and larvae if found. He also confirmed a suspicion that the Superintendent had begun to entertain himself; namely that his security check of buildings with a view over the show ground, though effective against normal forms of terrorism, was not appropriate in the case of the Blandford fly, which could home in on its target round corners. When this was pointed out it seemed obvious that the plotters would expect the police to search buildings with a direct view. The chance of discovery would be negligible if they hid their terror weapon in a flat with no field of fire over the show.

The search would have to be extended more widely. But unlike the immediate area, which had been investigated painstakingly over a period of weeks, and could be rechecked in a matter of hours, the surrounding streets were uncharted territory. And there was very little time.

To add to his troubles, Wilberforce was being pressurized by the RHS, which reminded him that many of its members had tickets for the following day, and ought to be kept informed. Could they not be told of the breakthrough in the police investigation?

Wilberforce tried not to sound irritated. 'I'm sure you'll see if you think about it that that's out of the question. If we find this nest of flies, we shall want to arrest whoever's there looking after them. To announce in advance that we're coming for them wouldn't be very clever.'

Meanwhile, the search went on. Rechecking premises overlooking the show ground took very little time, but the apartment blocks in neighbouring streets were a different matter. Many of the inhabitants were out on their daily business, and those who were at home tended, after the manner of flat-dwellers, to defend their privacy by knowing very little about their absent neighbours. As there was no question of breaking into flat after flat when the bell was not answered, most of the work would have to be left till the evening, when people came home from work.

On the advice of the expert, special attention was paid to a large apartment block near the bottom of Chelsea Bridge Road. It was screened off from the show ground by a belt of trees, which would provide natural gathering places for the males waiting to mate. But it contained over a hundred flats. By eleven that night three-quarters of them had been checked, and Detective Constables Jowett and Mercer were waiting outside one of the entrances to question late-comers as they went in. As they waited a taxi drew up and an elderly couple got out, a mild-faced old lady carrying a huge bunch of flowers and a shrivelled stick of a husband with a basket of vegetables. The detectives identified themselves and stated their business. The couple lived in one of the ground-floor flats, and had been spending the day with their married daughter in Surrey. Having thus accounted for themselves satisfactorily, they were asked if they knew the owner of the ground-floor flat next door to them, who was not at home.

'She's away, isn't she, Ada?' said the husband.

'That's right dear, a little holiday she told us. But—'

'Now, Ada, the police won't be interested in that. It's not the sort of thing they can do anything about.'

'You never know, dear. They might be able to.'

The detectives pricked up their ears and asked for details.

'Well, you see she's not young. Nearly forty, wouldn't you say, Charlie dear?'

'A bit long in the tooth, yes.'

'So when this young man moved in with her, years younger than her and very good-looking, we thought at first he must be just a lodger. But it wasn't that at all, she'd taken off her glasses and started using a lot of make-up and twice they came home together rather late at night, and she made a lot of noise in the hall as if she was tipsy.'

This needed investigating further. 'How long ago was it, madam, that the young man moved in?' asked Mercer.

She thought. 'Only about a fortnight. And then last week – when was it, Charlie?'

'Wednesday.'

'There they were out in the hall with their luggage waiting for a cab and she was all excited and showing off her wonderful new boyfriend to us and saying they were going away to Paris for a long weekend.'

The detectives exchanged glances. 'What did this young man look like?'

'Tall and ever so romantic looking,' sighed Ada, 'with lovely hazel eyes and a curly brown beard.'

'Up to no good,' Charlie grunted. 'Out to have the silly woman's money off her.'

'I don't think she has any, dear. She works in the Ministry of Agriculture. No one would do that if they were rich. But it's very worrying.'

115

'Yes, dear. But the police can't do anything about it, this is of no interest to them.'

On the contrary, the two young detectives were very interested indeed. Their briefing had included a description of a tall, handsome young man with a beard who was wanted for interview. Earlier in the case, he had been involved in a kidnapping in a village in Surrey.

'What sort of a beard?' Jowett asked.

'Tidy,' said Charlie. 'Cut into fancy shapes.'

It fitted the description they had been given. Trying not to sound excited, Jowett asked if anyone had had access to the flat since the pair went away.

'No . . .' Ada began.

'Yes,' contradicted Charlie.

'How could they, dear?' She turned to the detectives. 'You see we keep her spare key in case she gets locked out. If anyone needed to be let in, they'd have to collect it from us.'

'Ada, you've forgotten the men from the carpet-cleaning company who came with that great machine. She must have given them a key.'

'I reckon this is what we're looking for,' said Jowett. Agog with visions of rapid promotion, he reported to the incident room on his cellphone.

It was Grigg who took the call. 'Well done, lads, well done. We'll be with you in seconds.'

He and Wilberforce lost no time on the way. With them was the expert from Wareham and an assistant carrying a knapsack sprayer full of insecticide. On seeing this apparatus the elderly couple went wild with curiosity and had to be shooed back into their flat, told what was going on and sworn to secrecy. The preparations for the assault involved changing into the protective clothing that the expert had brought with him. Rather than let this happen in the hall where they would be exposed to the curiosity of residents arriving home late, Wilberforce set up his headquarters in the old couple's flat. Refusing pressing offers of cups of tea he, Grigg, and the two experts put on their protective clothing and returned to the entrance hall.

'We'll go in first,' said Wilberforce.

The expert queried this. 'Wouldn't you rather wait till we've dealt with the flies?'

'No!'

His vehemence had shocked the expert.

'Sorry,' he added. 'But there'll be an armed minder in there with them. We'll go first.'

As he loaded his firearm, the prospect of a shoot-out in a flat full of blood-sucking insects disgusted and alarmed him. But at the sight of Grigg swathed in protective clothing he managed a nervous laugh. 'I can think of nicer circumstances for making an arrest,' he said, adjusting his beekeeper's veil.

Grigg, who had suffered agonies already from the attentions of the Blandford fly, managed a feeble smile. 'Will this clobber really keep them out?'

Bracing himself, he unlocked the door of the flat with the spare key borrowed from the elderly couple. Wilberforce flattened himself against the wall and shouted 'Police! Come out with your hands up!'

Anticlimax. They were in a passage, with the doors of rooms opening off it. There were no flies, and so far, no gunman.

'Look, there they are!' cried the expert, pointing.

Above the door at the end of the passage was a pane of glass, with a mass of angry, struggling insects flattened against it on the other side.

Wilberforce flung open the door. The disgusting swarm, maddened at the prospect of blood, rushed through it to the attack. With insects all over him, probing for gaps in his defences, he repeated his call to the gunman to surrender.

There was no reply. Hampered by the insects brushing against their veils, he and Grigg conducted a cautious search. But there was no one there.

While the expert and his assistant got to work with the sprayer in the front room Wilberforce and Grigg withdrew to the entrance hall.

'Have to stake the place out for when they come back,' said Grigg.

117

'Yes. Someone senior ought to be here. You'd better stay, with the two constables.'

The constables were found drinking tea in the old couple's flat and basking in their admiration. Wilberforce gave them their orders, and added: 'I'm sorry to condemn you to a night in a flies' cemetery.'

'Not nearly as sorry as that poor woman will be when she gets back,' said Grigg. 'Let down by her gorgeous new boyfriend, and her flat knee deep in dead insects.'

The next task was to confront the RHS, which foreseeably wanted to tell its members that thanks to the police, the danger was over. It was furious when Wilberforce insisted that nothing could be said till an arrest had been made, and demanded to know why not.

Wilberforce was furious too. 'Have you any idea how many police man-hours have been tied up over this? We dislike so-called terrorists who waste our time, and we're determined to get them. I'm not prepared to give the peace of mind of your members priority over my chances of making an arrest. If I did, my people would mutiny.'

Still dissatisfied, the RHS appealed to higher authority over his head, and he was soon called to the phone in the incident room to speak to the Metropolitan Police Commissioner.

'But we'll have made an arrest by tomorrow morning, sir,' he protested, 'and we can make an announcement then. What does it matter if their members turn up a bit late? They've bought their tickets for the members' day in advance, the organizers won't lose money.'

'They say they've sold as many tickets as the ground will take and they're worried about overcrowding if a lot of people put off coming till the afternoon. We can't have old ladies trampled to death in the crush. One minute, Wilberforce, something's just come in.'

Wilberforce waited.

'The BBC has had a phone message from the Front,' said the Commissioner. 'All streets within a quarter-mile radius of the Chelsea ground are to be evacuated by eight

118

tomorrow morning, and kept clear of pedestrians and traffic till further notice.'

'And the BBC's proposing to broadcast that?' Wilberforce lamented.

'Hold on, I'll find out . . . well apparently the codeword was OK: St Finians, the one they used before, so it isn't a hoax. The normal drill is, we don't stop them warning the public of a threat if we're sure it's genuine.'

'But there's no threat. The flies are all dead, no one in the area is going to get bitten.'

'If we ask the BBC not to put it out, they'll find some newspaper that will. I'm inclined to let it go, and add a press release of our own. "The Metropolitan Police have made thorough enquiries into this matter and are satisfied that there is no danger to the public from visiting the Chelsea Flower Show. They do not intend to close any of the surrounding streets to traffic." How about that?'

'I don't like it, sir.'

'Why? Could there be another nest of flies somewhere else?'

'No, sir, we've checked everywhere. There can't be.'

'Then I think we'll put out a statement. We must say something. The horticultural people are really worried about their overcrowding problem. Besides, think of the plus for us when the poor bumbling police are proved right for once.'

'But we'll be warning the Front not to go back to the flat and be arrested.'

'I don't think so. They'll decide we're just being stupidly over-confident; we've taken every conceivable precaution against bombs, and haven't thought of other possibilities. But they underrated you, Wilberforce. Working that out was good thinking.'

'Not mine, sir. It was a suggestion from a member of the public.'

'Really? Who?'

'She is very anxious to avoid publicity, sir. I'd rather not say.'

119

'Then congratulate the anonymous lady warmly from me.'

After the call was over, an ugly thought struck Wilberforce. What if the Front had concocted a bomb as a second line of defence?

In the flat in Chelsea Bridge Road Grigg sat on a hard chair, well back from the window, and out of sight from the entrance door. He had created a fly-free zone round himself with the aid of a dustpan and brush. The two detective constables, who were taking turns with him on guard duty, were sleeping fully clothed on the absent lady's bed. In the bath was a revolting mess of hatched and unhatched pupae.

Watching the dawn break, Grigg wondered how soon their visitor would appear. His only task would be to open windows; a three-minute job which could be left till just before eight, the time which the Front had announced for the start of its operations. But people would be about by then. Anyone entering the flat in a beekeeper's veil and protective clothing would be very noticeable. Grigg had half expected someone to arrive under cover of darkness.

By the end of his watch it was broad daylight. Surely, he thought, something must happen soon. He decided to sit up with the constable who was due to relieve him. With an arrest imminent, it would be better to have a reception party of two.

Half-past six. They were all three awake now, and very tense. A brew of tea would have been welcome. But with dead flies everywhere in the kitchen, the idea nauseated them.

An hour later, Wilberforce came through from the incident room on the mobile phone. 'What's happening?'

'No action yet.'

'Hell. That press release of the Commissioner's must have frightened them off.'

'There's half an hour to go yet.'

'Left it a bit late, haven't they? Let me know when it happens.'

'Will do.'

Soon people were walking past the window towards the entrance to the Flower Show. A trickle at first, but soon they were streaming past, arriving early to beat the crowds. The Commissioner's press release seemed to have had a reassuring effect. It even looked as if some of the people were gapers, uninterested in horticulture, who had come along on the off-chance, hoping to see a disaster.

Eight o'clock came. Grigg picked up the mobile phone to report failure.

Then it happened. Three powerful motorcycles came roaring along the street from the direction of Sloane Square. The riders wore helmets and masks covering most of their faces. So did the three pillion passengers. As they rode past, each of them raised a hand and hurled a large brick with unerring aim through the window of the flat. The hole was enormous, an army of flies could have escaped through it. The detectives were showered with broken glass.

'Bloody hell!' cried Grigg, and reached for the mobile telephone.

Anxious to cover all eventualities, Wilberforce had stationed an unmarked police car out of sight round the corner in Ebury Street. Alerted by the noise, it set off at once in pursuit. But he had not reckoned with motorcycles, which could weave their way through traffic faster than any car. As they roared away along the Embankment they scattered leaflets on the pavement among the RHS members walking towards the Bullring entrance to the show. The police car gave chase at once, and kept them in sight as they crossed the Thames at the Albert Bridge. But in the crowded streets of Battersea it lost them and Wilberforce's hopes of making an arrest were at an end.

According to several witnesses, the helmet of one of the brick-throwing pillion passengers had a pony-tail of fair hair protruding from under the back of it. But current taste in unisex hairdressing made it unsafe to conclude that its owner was female.

Seven

By mid-afternoon Celia was back at Archerscroft inspecting a batch of *Cyclamen libanoticum* for signs of mite infestation. She had spent the previous night at her club, listening avidly to newscasts which told her less than she knew already. The news of the Green Front's defeat did not break till nine in the morning. The item was followed by an impromptu press conference by Wilberforce in which, to her horror, he confessed modestly that the credit was not wholly his. The suggestion that the Blandford fly might be the Front's secret terror weapon had come from 'a member of the public'. Pressed to give details he said that the person concerned disliked publicity and did not wish to be named. But under intensive questioning he became entangled in personal pronouns and let slip that the member of the public was 'she' and not 'he'.

Feeling like a hunted member of an endangered species, Celia fled, to put as many miles as possible between herself and Chelsea. Too many of her colleagues in the RHS knew of her Miss Marple tendencies. If they saw her around they might put two and two together, with results which did not bear thinking about.

Next day she bought all the morning papers and scanned them, fearful of finding herself identified. To her relief she was not mentioned. But a lady entomologist in Bristol who had been fastened on as a possible candidate had come home from her laboratory to find a disorderly press rabble encamped on her front lawn.

The expert from Wareham was much in evidence on

122

the feature pages, expounding the life-cycle of the Bland-ford fly. The quality broadsheets were rather stuffy in their condemnation of the Green Front, which they accused of having tried to wreck an important national occasion and make an impertinent assault on the dignity of the RHS and its distinguished membership. Brutal violence, all the papers insisted, was not the way to promote the ecological cause. They went on to prove themselves wrong by publicizing all the issues raised in the leaflets scattered by the motorcyclists outside the ground. A mass of feature articles stressed the danger of letting agricultural and horticultural chemicals run off into watercourses, and deplored the wholesale extraction of peat from Britain's few remaining wetlands. Pundits of all persuasions gave their opinion. The Peat Producers' Association made soothing remarks about its concern for conservation, firms dealing in substitutes for peat managed to ensure that their wares received favourable mention, and environmentalists uttered their cries of doom. One of the tabloids maintained that the RHS and its middle-class membership deserved to be jolted out of their complacency over environmental issues. In the paper's view, with which Celia had a sneaking sympathy, the Front's ingenious plan of attack deserved to succeed.

Back from the triumph of his silver medal, the Admiral had invited what he called 'my companions in arms at Chelsea' to a celebratory drink that evening. Celia felt obliged to put in an appearance and found the assembled company standing about among the crowded ornaments and niggly little flowerbeds of his back garden. It was a larger party than she had expected. As well as the Chelsea team, the groupies, Wilfrid Edgeley and Mrs Cadogan, were also present.

The Admiral greeted Celia warmly. 'Welcome, my dear, welcome. It was your nursery which furnished me with the raw materials with which I built our success, I shall never forget that. Let me get you a restorative. A whisky, perhaps.'

123

She opted for sherry, for the Admiral's whiskies were almost lethally potent. It looked as if he had already administered more than one of them to himself.

'For me, a garden is nothing if it is not spacious,' he boomed unsteadily, surveying his cluttered half-acre with pride. 'After the cramping confinement of that little courtyard at Chelsea, a scene like this comes as a blessed relief.'

As the expected compliments on his garden were produced, he made a defiant gesture towards the far end, where an open post and rail fence allowed the uninformed to conclude that Baker's Meadow, which lay beyond it, was also part of his property. 'I do not intend to have my peace disturbed,' he added, 'and my sight offended by rows of obscene executive houses, so called, on the far side of that fence for commuters to infest. Oh, no. Mister jumped-up barrow-boy Fortescue has another think coming.'

He took another long swig at his whisky and went on in a confidential mutter. 'Brutal philistinism will not triumph. The Historic Buildings Survey has already come down in favour of my application.' He fell silent, having apparently decided that no further explanation was needed.

Mrs Cadogan stepped into the communications breach. 'The wretched Fortescue has managed to buy two of the houses in the High Street that back on to Baker's Meadow—'

'And thrown the unfortunate inhabitants out into the street,' trumpeted the Admiral on a note of lugubrious pity.

'Well, he offered them much better houses elsewhere,' she corrected. 'And of course he wants to knock them down and make an entrance to Baker's Meadow in the gap.'

The Admiral cackled gleefully. 'But there won't be a gap. The inspector is coming tomorrow morning. By nightfall all those houses will be under a preservation order as historic buildings that can't be demolished. That vandalizing Visigoth won't be able to get anything bigger than a bicycle into that field past them, let alone his filthy lorry-loads of bricks. Baker's Meadow will be safe from him.'

It was an ingenious scheme, and Celia wondered which of them, him or Mrs Cadogan, had thought of it. That end of the High Street was lined with pleasant little houses dating mostly from the early nineteenth century. Singly they were not of enormous historic interest. As a group they formed part of a picturesque old-world streetscape. It would be a sin to knock any of them down.

The Admiral, intent on having the beauties of his garden admired, proposed a conducted tour. But vaguely sinister noises had been coming for some time from the direction of the High Street, and as they advanced down the garden they became louder, resolving themselves into a roar of heavy machinery, punctuated from time to time by crashing sounds as of falling masonry. Everyone rushed to the fence and the Admiral, rigid with indignation, let out a strangled cry. On the far side of the field there was a gap where two of the houses had been, and in the gap a bulldozer was rampaging in a rising cloud of dust. Fortescue had beaten the preservation order by a margin of a few hours.

The Admiral was first over the fence, breathing fury and whisky fumes and almost falling flat on his face on the far side. The others followed, full of concern. He was beside himself, unless prevented he might well throw himself under the bulldozer or try to murder its driver. But as the party streamed across the grass, a thickset man in his fifties emerged from the ruin of the two cottages and advanced to meet them. He wore his yachting cap at a jaunty angle and his air of solid self-confidence had behind it a fortune numbered in billions and a history of successful takeover bids linking five continents. He was flanked by a secretary with a briefcase and three plug-ugly bully-boys: the bodyguards who accompanied him everywhere at home and abroad.

'Fortescue, what the hell d'you think you're doing?' the Admiral roared.

No emotion appeared on the tycoon's pudgy bulldog

face. His cold eyes were fixed on the Admiral, but he said nothing.

'How dare you . . . desecrate our national heritage?' bellowed the Admiral, suppressing a hiccup. 'You flout the law, you ignore every principle of moral and aesthetic decency. But you will pay dearly for this outrage, which only a person of subhuman intelligence and no sensibility at all would have dared to commit. You are vermin, sir, your very existence is offensive. The united wish of everyone in this village is that you should disappear back down the pest-ridden rat hole from which you emerged to plague us. There is no place for scum such as you here.'

Ignoring him, Fortescue said curtly, 'Wilson, deal with this.'

The secretary advanced on the Admiral and held out some papers, as if to explain the legal position. The Admiral snatched them from him and ground them underfoot in the grass.

'Pick up those papers,' said Fortescue calmly. 'No, not you, Wilson, I want him to pick them up.'

When the Admiral made no move, two of the bully-boys came forward and advanced menacingly towards him. To defuse the situation James Carstairs picked up the papers and handed them to Wilson, while the Admiral swayed on his feet and muttered in inarticulate rage.

Celia was transfixed with horror. What Fortescue had done was unforgivable, the houses fronting the High Street would have a gap in them like a missing front tooth. The Admiral was behaving foolishly, but her heart bled for him. He was a tragic, not a comic figure.

Fortescue addressed the company in general. 'And now will you get off my land, all of you. You're trespassing.'

The Admiral recovered his voice. 'We are not trespassing,' he shouted. 'There is a public right of way across this field.'

'The path is up at the other end,' said Fortescue coldly, 'and when you thought you owned the land you were telling everyone it didn't exist. Are you going to move or are you not?'

126

'We stand united on our legal rights,' cried the Admiral, glancing round at his companions for support. Mrs Cadogan turned to Celia with a helpless gesture. They had to give it him though they knew he was putting himself in the wrong.

A large, angry crowd had gathered in the street on the far side of the heap of rubble. Youths among it had started shouting abuse at Fortescue. His two heavies advanced again threateningly towards the Admiral. But he motioned them back. A policeman was standing by, ready to intervene if the situation got out of hand.

'The old fool's drunk,' said Fortescue. 'Wilson, fetch that policeman.'

The policeman, a local constable whom the Admiral knew well, approached him and took him aside. 'This is a bad business, sir, and we all know how you feel. You're not the only one that's upset, but we have to keep the peace, don't we? And when the gentleman asks you to leave his land, he's within his rights.'

'He's not a gentleman, my dear fellow. Don't talk such nonsense.'

'I'm sorry, sir, but it's not nonsense. You and your friends are on private land where you have no right to be. It's my duty to ask you to leave.'

'You are a Judas, Constable,' intoned the Admiral in a martyred voice. 'I thought better of you.'

He stood there, swaying slightly, while the constable went on reasoning with him quietly. After a time he nodded, and began to advance towards the wreckage of the cottages.

'George, where are you going?' cried Mrs Cadogan sharply.

'I must speak to the people, give them the leadership they cry out for.' He began to climb the heap of rubble, apparently intending to address the crowd from the top.

'No, George. Come back.'

'But they will expect it of me.'

'He mustn't, he's much too drunk,' muttered Mrs Cadogan. 'Wilfrid, go and make him come back.'

Tottering among the foothills of the rubble mountain,

the Admiral himself seemed to realize that he was in no
fit state to scale it, and let Edgeley help him back to
safety.

'Come, George, it's time to go home,' said Mrs
Cadogan.

Angry and humiliated, he let himself be led away across
the field. The others followed. Celia was deeply sorry for
him. The affront to his dignity was bad enough without
the added hurt of knowing that he had brought it on
himself by his idiotic behaviour to Margaret Fortescue.
She was amazed, too, by Fortescue's conduct. He had
the reputation of being a ruthless international business-
man. She had vague memories of a feud with another
firm some years ago, which had been pursued through
the courts right up to the House of Lords. But it was
astonishing that a multi-millionaire with world-wide
interests to look after should find the time and energy to
wreak revenge for an insult to his wife by master-minding
a tuppenny-ha'penny development scheme which was
bound to make him bitterly unpopular in his home village.
What, she wondered, did his wife think about it? Had
she tried to dissuade him? How did a woman remain well
balanced with a husband who was a bullying, grudge-
bearing brute?

Back in the Admiral's garden farewells amid condol-
ences had begun. But he was preoccupied with a problem
which had occurred to him as the effects of the whisky
wore off. How had Fortescue found out that the building
inspector was due to pronounce on the aesthetic merits
of the two houses next morning?

'It is a tragic thought which wounds me deeply,' he
moaned, glancing round. 'But I have been betrayed, we
have a traitor, a spy in our midst.'

Everyone exclaimed in horror at this suggestion, but
Celia decided that he must be right. No one would bring
in a demolition team at seven in the evening unless they
knew that action next day would be too late. But who
had told Fortescue that he needed to act at once?

*

While this drama was played out in Melbury, Superintendent Wilberforce had been furiously busy, spurring on his team to fresh efforts. His failure to make arrests after the Chelsea fiasco had only strengthened his determination to find and arrest the people who had cocked a snook at public order and wasted enormous amounts of police time.

'That Irishman,' he mused in one of his conferences with Grigg. 'He talked without an Irish accent to that very bright Sergeant Plod in Dorset.'

'So he's an Irishman who can sound English when he wants to.'

'Or an Englishman who can frighten us by sounding Irish.'

'Whichever he is,' said Wilberforce, 'he has inside IRA knowledge. There's that code-word, remember. And the detonators. But which side of the fence did he acquire it?'

'Ah. I see what you mean, Super. He could be one of our own undercovers gone wrong.'

'Exactly.'

It was a tenable theory. The whole Northern Ireland scene was utterly corrupt, full of double agents and protection rackets and murders committed for unspeakable non-political reasons. If their Irishman was an Army spy who had slipped over the edge into crime, he would not have been the first one to do so.

'Want me to go back to Belfast?' Grigg asked. 'Go through the records again?'

'Yes. And keep a sharp lookout for an undercover who was phased out four or five years ago, while St Finians was still current as a code-word and those detonators we found at Keeper's Cottage were still standard IRA issue.'

Next morning he and Padstow set off into Cambridgeshire on what he suspected was a fool's errand. A small nursery near Newmarket had been burnt down during the night. The local force suspected that the owners, who were heavily in debt to their bank, had torched it themselves to collect the insurance. Wilberforce had every reason to hope that this was so. He was convinced that the Green Front had existed only to perpetrate the hoax at Chelsea and had no intention of mounting a continuing terror campaign.

Turning off the motorway at the Newmarket exit, and following directions given them by the local force, they soon came on what they were looking for: a small nursery and garden centre in a devastated state. Almost every pane in the glasshouses was smashed. Smoke was still rising from the ashes of the sales building. The picture was completed by two police cars and the demoralized youngish couple whose business had just been wrecked.

'What happened?' Wilberforce asked the inspector in charge.

'They say all hell broke loose just after midnight. Their bungalow's just across the road. They were woken because some men roared up on motorcycles and started breaking the glass in the greenhouses. Then they bashed in the door of the sales building and set fire to it. Apparently it was all over in minutes.'

The distressed owners had joined them and were nodding agreement with this account.

'Why don't you two go indoors and make yourselves a cup of tea?' the Inspector suggested. 'We'll join you later.'

'You're not happy?' Wilberforce queried when they had gone.

'Well, there are some suspicious aspects. They say it happened just after twelve, but the electric clock by the cash desk didn't stop till just after one. They say they must have misread the time in their panic. They also say the attackers bashed down the doors of the sales building to get in. But those doors are quite heavy; a motorcycle couldn't do it. When we told them that they changed their story and said they thought there'd been a van as well. They admit that they're up to their necks in debt, mostly to their bank. And the bank's been pressing them.'

Wilberforce was relieved. 'So it's a copycat job? They think they can blame it on the Green Front, in the aftermath of the publicity over Chelsea?'

'That's what it looks like.'

But even as Wilberforce spoke he had doubts. 'If Chelsea was a one-off, and they've torched the place themselves for the insurance, they can't stop there, an attack on one small garden centre isn't enough. They've got to establish that the Green Front is still on the warpath with an ongoing campaign of destruction up and down the country. Can you see these two torching garden centres right left and centre to make their insurance claim stick?'

'If you're desperate, with the bank breathing down your neck, you don't always think things out all that clearly.'

Wilberforce would have liked to believe this for the sake of his own peace of mind. 'What does the fire service say?'

'Their arson man hasn't been yet. He's on his way.' The Inspector produced a sheet of paper from his briefcase. 'We found this pinned to a tree.'

The message was crudely printed in block capitals with a felt pen:

This shop sells peat cut from a Site of Special Scientific Interest, also slug pellets containing methiocarb, which is even more toxic than methaldehyde, and lindane, which is suspected of causing cancer and genetic damage. It is therefore a legitimate target and has been treated as such.

The Fighters of the Green Front.

'Oh, and this was with it,' said the Inspector, and handed Wilberforce a copy of a printed leaflet. It was identical with the leaflets that had appeared everywhere in the run-up to Chelsea.

'They could have picked one of these up anywhere,' said Wilberforce.

Vaguely consoled by this thought, he set off towards London against the outward flow of the evening commuter traffic. But the consolation did not last.

As they entered the northern suburbs police headquarters in Cambridge came through on the phone. The

Green Front had contacted them and claimed responsibility for the attack, quoting a code-word: St Finians. Wilberforce was aghast. The Green Front was still in business. Chelsea had not been a one-off after all.

A piece of news which greeted him back in the office plunged him even deeper into gloom. Five fire bombs planted in a large garden centre in Hertfordshire had gone off at intervals during the day, and the police were still hunting for more. They had done little damage. Nevertheless, a campaign of violence against horticultural establishments up and down the country had begun, with no means of knowing where the next target would be.

Grigg, hot on the trail of the blue-chinned Irishman, was paying his second visit to a room full of men intent on their computer terminals, very similar to the registries in regional crime squad headquarters all over the United Kingdom. But this one was in Belfast. The men were soldiers and the information stored in the computer was not about the sordid day-to-day transactions of the criminal world, but about the murderous undercover war waged by the Army against fanatics on either side of the Catholic–Protestant divide.

'You again?' said Philip Molesey, the sergeant who presided over the room. 'Still on the Blandford fly thing? Cor, insect bites count as terrorism on your side of the water, do they?'

'It's fire bombs now, worse luck. I've come to run another check.'

'Why? New lead?'

'That's right. Our joker's been reported speaking Standard English. The Super thinks it's one of our old undercovers gone wild, trying to frighten us with an Irish accent and a bit of IRA credibility.'

'What sort of Irish accent? A proper southern brogue, or just working-class Ulster?'

'We don't know. It could have been neither, just an Englishman's attempt to imitate what the Irish sound like. Both the witnesses who heard him do it were English.'

'If he was an undercover, he wouldn't last long unless he was word perfect.'

132

'Assume he was, shall we, for the moment? Narrow it down a bit.'

'Yes. Let's have a look-see.'

The computer screen threw up a list of men whom the Army had used to infiltrate terrorist organizations and provide information about their activities. After each name was a brief summary: active between such and such dates, compromised and killed by Provisionals, or in the luckier cases compromised and phased out, which meant that the man had been given a new identity in Canada or Australia. A tap or two on the keyboard eliminated all but the few Standard English speakers, mostly Army officers with an Irish element in their background. Of these five were dead. Only four were in the 'compromised and phased out' category. Molesey typed in each name in turn, summoning to the screen the details of an active service career: date and place of birth, education, service record, and finally the circumstances in which the person had been withdrawn from undercover activity. In one case this happened because the man had been manoeuvred into a position where he could only have maintained his credibility by committing an atrocious murder in Protestant North Belfast. In another, an unlucky accident had exposed his cover. The third had been withdrawn because he got sidetracked into a world of corruption and money-grabbing intrigue which had little to do with sectarian politics.

The fourth officer on the list was Michael Hamilton. He had been born in county Cork in 1961 and educated at St Mary's College, Cork, after which he had joined the British Army. But at this point the record ended abruptly with the words 'further information in special index'.

'Oh-oh, he's in the poison cupboard,' said Molesey. 'Something extra nasty there.'

'I like it,' said Grigg. 'Who has the key to the poison cupboard?'

'Colonel Timmins, Grenadier Guards. Bit of a stickler. You have to show good cause.'

'Fire-bombing is good cause.'

133

'I'll take you along to him then.'

The Colonel occupied a small office on the next floor. He was not forthcoming at first, but the mention of fire bombs worked as an open sesame, and he became co-operative. 'What does your chap look like?'

Grigg told him.

Colonel Timmins reached behind him to a filing cabinet and pulled out a file with a passport-size photograph attached. 'That's Hamilton. Any resemblance?'

'Could be. It corresponds to the description and photofit.'

'Nasty-looking little Irish runt, isn't he? No need for me to look up the file, I remember him only too well after the dance he led us.'

'How did he come to join the British Army if he was born in the South?'

'Anglo-Irish on his father's side. Protestant ascendancy at its last gasp. Charles I was trying to raise money and sold them an earldom, but they've come down in the world. The Fenians burnt the house to the ground in the Troubles, but the family pigged it in the stables and managed to keep the land. Michael's father had some kind of job as an auctioneer, so they were able to send him to St Mary's College.'

'But that sounds like a Catholic school. You said the father was Protestant ascendancy.'

'Ah, but the mother wasn't. He'd married a Catholic and of course the priests insisted on the boy being brought up in her religion. I'm told she was a real Irish beauty, as mad as they come, and that's where he got his devilment from.'

'And his brogue.'

'That's right.'

'And how did he make out in the Army?'

'He was in the Falklands campaign and did well. The trouble started after that, when he was posted here and transferred to the SAS as an undercover. And from that point on, oh dear. Everything went wrong.'

'What in particular?' Grigg asked.

134

'To start with, he was an arch-fornicator. One of those wiry little men who worm their way into women's beds while the gorgeous great hunks are left standing. And he collected scalps, for a laugh. His colonel's wife, for instance. Not because she was pretty, she wasn't, unless you consider a hippopotamus pretty. But she was his colonel's wife, so it was worth collecting her scalp. And if anyone ran into him in Belfast when he was supposed to be sweating it out on the border in South Armagh, he always had a plausible story to explain why.'

'But operationally, how did he do?'

'He was brilliant at first. Got himself infiltrated into the IRA in no time at all, started pulling in first-class information. Then we got worried. Some of the stuff he turned in sounded too good to be true, especially when it was information we couldn't use or even check without blowing his cover. At one time there was a theory that the Provisionals were running him as a double agent, but that was never proved. And he had this wild sense of humour, some of his so-called operations were little more than practical jokes involving enormous risks and a lot of lying. What we did know was, he was getting far too deep in. We don't worry if an undercover goes into action with a detachment that's going to commit an IRA atrocity, they have to do that occasionally to maintain their credibility, but Mike Hamilton went far beyond that, he let them send him on murder missions by himself.'

'Dead against the rules,' Grigg commented.

'And presently we began to suspect that they weren't IRA missions, but gang warfare murder jobs in the fight between rival rackets, you know what a sink of corruption this place is. We got more and more worried, and in the end he did something so mad and silly that we had to pull him out.'

He ran a hand through his sparse hair and went on. 'He got involved in a very tidy little protection racket, run by the Provisionals in collaboration with their enemies on the Protestant side, splitting the money fifty-fifty. If you had a business and paid up, the Provos guaranteed that your factory wouldn't be blown up and your management wouldn't have to look under the car every morning, and the Protestant paramilitaries promised not to shoot up the Catholics in your work-force. It worked perfectly till someone killed the managing director of a firm that had paid up regularly. Of course that was against all the rules of honourable sectarian combat, and the two sides began accusing each other of bad faith. We happened to have an undercover in place watching all this, and he turned in pretty conclusive evidence that Hamilton was responsible.'

'Why did he do it? He must have been mad.'

'How right you are. It was anyone's guess which lot would tear him to pieces first. Of course we couldn't let him be charged with murder, much as we'd have liked to, he knew too much and it would have meant exhibiting a lot of dirty military linen in court. So we just smuggled him out to the mainland damn quick.'

'And gave him a cover identity?'

'No, we decided he could damn well do that for himself. He'd made a pile out of his various skulduggeries while he was here, and we saw no reason to help.'

'You haven't by any chance got an address?'

Colonel Timmins consulted the file. 'Sorry, no. All it says here is, he's believed to have emigrated to Australia. He must have come back if your identification's right.'

'I think it probably is. The character fits, it's the same sense of humour. Lots of trickery and complicated plot-weaving, and if anyone gets killed it's just too bad.'

'How about the fornication?'

'That fits too, he was caught hard at it with a blonde by a village policeman in Dorset. One other thing. You've no idea why he killed that managing director?'

'Not really. We think it was probably a well-paid contract killing. You'd like a copy of his mug-shot, I imagine.'

'Please. Several if you can manage it.'

Wilberforce had unfinished business to attend to in Melbury, and took the photographs of Hamilton there

136

himself. All the witnesses agreed that this was the man they had seen. This was a step forward. But all he had was a firm identity for a man whose whereabouts he did not know, probably living under an alias, who was almost certainly busy packing fire bombs into a holdall ready for the Green Front's next victim, who could be anywhere in the United Kingdom. That did not get one very far.

One thing puzzled Wilberforce. Hamilton had taken advantage of Northern Ireland's climate of corruption to lay the foundations of a promising criminal career. Why had he abandoned blackmail or fraud or whatever it was that he did for a living and taken to the violent defence of the environment instead?

Celia, fearful of blowing her cover, had refused to come to Welstead police station to make the identification. 'If I keep running in and out of the place, people will wonder why. Could we meet at a quiet country pub somewhere instead?'

Wilberforce agreed, and they met at the Green Dragon in Madingley. It was his first chance to talk to her since Chelsea. He bought her a large gin, thanked her again rather formally for the inspired guess which had saved the day there, then went on to put a question. 'What do you know about a man called Wilfrid Edgeley? Is he a green enthusiast by any chance?'

'Goodness no. He belongs to the Garden Society, but only as an excuse to get away from his very bossy wife.'

'Then you don't think he could be masterminding a cell of the Green Front in Melbury?'

She burst out laughing. 'Wilfrid is incapable of masterminding a coffee morning for church funds. His wife bullies him mercilessly. If anyone's doing any masterminding, it's her.'

'No, Mrs Grant. She's a non-starter, if it's either of them it's him.'

'That's out of the question, honestly. Why on earth do you suspect him?'

'Because there's a link between him and your Monica Porter.'

'Really? What sort of a link?'

'I really oughtn't to tell you this, so please be very discreet. Our investigations have established that she's Edgeley's mistress.'

'Goodness me. How very surprising.'

'Is it?'

'On second thoughts, no. He's brainless and weak-kneed, but he's also very decorative. One can see that a masterful woman like Monica might go for him as a toy-boy. D'you think she bullies him as brutally as she bullies me?'

'I think being brutally bullied is the main attraction from his point of view.'

'Oh. You mean tyings to the bed and beatings?'

'Yes. The poor young detective constable who reported it was very shocked.'

'Mrs Edgeley is a Justice of the Peace and a head-mistress and the dominant partner at home, but she isn't the sort of lady who would oblige with that sort of caper. I can see why Wilfrid likes it, and Monica would enjoy dishing it out.'

He nodded. 'As you say, Edgeley is very good-looking, one can imagine a certain type of woman falling for him. Our people think it's a genuine love affair on both sides.'

'Is that why she moved down from London? To be near him?'

'Presumably.'

'Not so that she could spy on me for the Green Front?'

'No. So we're faced with a problem, aren't we?'

Celia was appalled. 'Horrors. I see what you mean.'

'Yes. If she isn't the spy, who is it?'

'Goodness knows.'

'I was hoping you'd come up with a suggestion. There must be someone. Who?'

'I'm sorry. I wish I could help you. I have absolutely no idea.'

Eight

According to Mrs Grant the Tidmarshes were back at their home base, and Wilberforce had a bone to pick with them. Intensive detective enquiries in environmental circles had shown that a man answering Hamilton's description had been at one of the conferences they had attended, and had been seen in conversation with them. It was time for a showdown.

'Cor, what a mess,' said Padstow as they drove into the smallholding.

The gate was off its hinges. The drive had been repaired by dumping piles of bricks in the deep potholes. A goat tethered with a ragged rope was nibbling at the remains of a disease-ridden rose bed. A wire enclosure, with holes in it blocked by pieces of hardboard, had evidently been intended as a hen-run, but most of the hens were outside. Stepping over a collection of rusty pails on the doorstep of the cottage, Wilberforce rattled the cowbell hanging in the porch.

Wendy appeared, in a dirty cotton dress. 'Oh, it's you. What d'you want now?'

'You and your husband have not told me the truth, and I propose to take you both to Welstead police station and question you under the provisions of the Prevention of Terrorism Act.'

She put on a superior smile and prepared to play games. 'Leaving our livestock unattended? You can't, Edward must stay here to look after them while you question me.'

'No.'

'In that case I shall file a complaint against you for cruelty to animals.'

'That won't be necessary, because I shall leave you here while I take Mr Tidmarsh away for interrogation.'

Suddenly animal welfare assumed a very low priority. She clearly shared Wilberforce's view that Edward would be the easier nut to crack, and did not want to let him out of her sight. But it was too late for her to backtrack and leave the animals to their lonely fate. Edward, fortified by exhortations to be brave in the face of police brutality, was bundled into the car and driven off to Welstead.

Facing him across the table in a bleak interviewing room, Wilberforce prepared to generate an appropriate atmosphere of intimidating menace. 'Now, Mr Tidmarsh. I don't like terrorism and I don't like people in contact with terrorism who lie to me. You haven't told me the truth, and I propose to keep you sitting here under the provisions of the Act till you do.'

Edward gave him a defensive smile from behind his crooked steel-framed glasses. 'Do calm down, there's no need to be like that. I don't share Wendy's belief that all policemen are wicked bullies, and as far as I know we haven't done anything illegal. So I'm perfectly happy to tell you everything I know.'

'That's OK then,' said Wilberforce, trying not to sound wrong-footed.

'So where shall I begin?'

Wilberforce produced a photograph. 'By telling me if you recognize this man.'

'Of course. That's Michael Vallance.'

'Correct. That's the alias he used at the conference in Eastbourne where you met him last autumn. His real name's Michael Hamilton. What brought him to your attention?'

'Well, everyone there was being a bit gloomy about the ozone layer, but he got a sort of grim doomsday fun out of it and made us all laugh.'

'And what part did he play in planning the Chelsea business?'

'He was the ringleader.'

'So the Blandford fly was his idea.'

'Oh, no! He muscled in on the act much later.'

'Then whose idea was it?'

'I don't know. We weren't told because the man has some kind of official position and has to be protected, but he's a biologist who put up the idea to Martin Grainger at the Organic Commune and we took it on from there.'

'When you say "we" who do you mean?'

'It started with a small group of us, all people connected directly or indirectly with the commune. We all hate the way people manicure and titivate their gardens and cut their lawns with stinking noisy motor mowers till they look like billiard tables and slosh poisonous chemicals about everywhere and smother everything with peat, which is a finite non-renewable resource, and avoid having compost heaps because they're an eyesore. We thought those people needed to be shaken out of their dreadful suburban garden-mania, and this suggestion of a practical joke at Chelsea seemed a very good idea. Nothing very ambitious, just a few dozen pupae dropped into ornamental pools and so on, and we were going to hand out some leaflets. But that was before Michael came along.'

'Ah. How did Hamilton fit in?'

'He heard about it and latched on. He was very dynamic, wanted us to raise our sights and mount something more ambitious, I think he must have been some kind of publicity expert. He had this idea that we should spread rumours beforehand about the dreadful terrorist outrage we were going to commit at Chelsea, and he arranged for caches of detonators and so on to be left around, and concocted subtle little plots to make sure they were found, so that the police would take the threat seriously. We got rather alarmed. Our tiny little idea had grown out of all recognition, it was as if someone had planted a cuckoo's egg on us, and we were having to feed this enormous creature instead of our own chick.'

'Why did you let him manipulate you all into tagging along?'

'Well, you see, Michael is one of those charismatic people, a sort of Pied Piper who can make you dance to his tune and think it enormous fun. He just carried us along with what he wanted us to do, making it seem a huge joke.'

'Even when it came to threatening death and destruction at Chelsea unless the show was cancelled?'

'Goodness, no. By that stage the whole business had been taken out of our hands. Michael was running the whole operation without consulting us. He'd got people of his own on the job, those sinister yobbos on motorcycles. We didn't get a look in. We were horrified, we'd no idea that he intended to release so many of the flies, or that he intended to carry on the campaign after Chelsea, with his yobbos smashing up garden centres and so on. That was nothing to do with us.'

'But it didn't occur to you to tell the police what you knew?'

'I thought we should, because terrorism's not funny. And I didn't see why not, because we'd done nothing illegal. That is, unless you count distributing a leaflet or two. But the whole commune was against me, they insisted that the brutal corrupt police would plant evidence on us and make up confessions and get us all long sentences as terrorists. As you've probably noticed, Wendy thinks along those lines, and when she's got the bit between her teeth there's no arguing with her.'

'I'm glad one of you had some sense of public duty.'

'Not much. I should have volunteered earlier.'

'I won't hold it against you, Mr Tidmarsh. Now about these subtle little plots to make sure the detonators and so on were found. You realize that he involved Mrs Grant in one of them?'

'Yes. We both felt rather bad about that. We like her.'

'Nevertheless you pointed her out to Hamilton as a possibility?'

'No. He asked us about her. He seemed to know quite a lot about her already. We didn't realize till much later why he wanted to know.'

142

That brought Wilberforce up short. Who had briefed Hamilton? Someone living in Melbury, or with connections there, but who? That would have to be thought about later.

'What sort of things did he ask you about?'

'What she was like. And about Mr Wilkins. He seemed to think Mr Wilkins was her lover, and said she made rather a fool of herself, dashing about and detecting madly to get him acquitted on the murder charge, while the police quietly got on with their job and arrested another man.'

'And did you confirm him in this view of Mrs Grant's character?'

'I said I didn't know, I'd seen no sign of a sex thing between her and Wilkins. But when he asked if Wilkins had a girlfriend, I had to say no, he was rather notorious for not having one, though he certainly wasn't gay.'

'And what else did he ask you?'

'He wanted to know the set-up in her office, whether she shared it with her secretary or not. I think that was all.'

'And all this happened during the conference at Eastbourne.'

'That's right. And when it got nearer the time Hamilton said he wanted us to go to the commune and help out.'

'And you arranged for Annabel Johnson to stand in for you here.'

'No. We'd fixed up for a girl from Friendly Cousins to come, someone we'd had before. But at the last moment it was all cancelled and the Johnson woman turned up instead.'

'Who fixed that?'

'I think Michael must have done.'

'What d'you know about her?'

'Nothing much. We didn't like her, she gave me the creeps.'

The same instinctive reaction, Wilberforce noted, as Mrs Grant's.

'Any forwarding address for her?' he asked.

143

'No. And she didn't know much about animals. We had to show her how to milk a goat.'

'But you'd arranged for this girl you knew to come,' said Wilberforce. 'Why d'you think Hamilton wanted to put in his own nominee instead?'

Edward shrugged. 'I've no idea.'

As Wilberforce pondered this question, a possible answer occurred to him. But it needed checking. He phoned forensics at the Yard for assistance, then drove Edward back to the smallholding, where Wendy examined him anxiously for bruises and asked him what he had been 'made to say'.

'Mr Tidmarsh has volunteered some valuable information,' said Wilberforce severely. 'If he had not done so I would have arrested you both for failing to report a crime. I shall now question you about it.'

Tiresomely, she tried to avoid answering his questions till she knew what Edward had said, so that she could say the same thing. The interrogation took a long time, and nothing new emerged. It was late afternoon when the team he had asked for from forensics arrived, to go through the Tidmarshes' cottage from top to bottom: no easy task, for there was disorder everywhere. They were looking for any trace that Annabel Johnson might have left behind, especially her fingerprints.

Wendy protested that Annabel had been gone for days. 'You won't find any prints now.'

The forensic team refrained politely from pointing out that fingerprints had a long life-expectancy in a house where nothing had been polished for years.

The Tidmarshes' prints were everywhere. But so were those of a third person. Wilberforce was relieved. He had feared that Johnson might have worn gloves throughout her stay in the house.

The electronics engineer he had summoned arrived shortly after the others. 'Evening, Super. What am I looking for?'

'The receiving end of an ultra-short-wave eavesdropping set-up. The target was the office building in the nursery garden next door.'

144

'Well within range. I'll have a look round.'

But after a thorough search, he reported that he had found nothing.

'How about outside, in a tree?'

'No. I've looked everywhere.'

'I'm not surprised. They had lots of time to dismantle it.'

'How about the other end, Super?'

'That's more likely, they wouldn't be able to get access. Let's try there.'

He crossed the road to Mrs Grant's cottage and knocked. 'I'm sorry to put your anonymity at risk, but we need to get into your office.'

'There's not much risk. The business shuts at five, so there's no one there. Why, though?'

'Microphones. An eavesdropping set-up run by Annabel Johnson.'

'Ah. Of course. Why on earth didn't I think of that when you said Monica Porter was out of it?'

'I ask myself the same question,' replied Wilberforce grimly. 'I should have realized that this might be quite a high-tech operation.'

She went with him and unlocked the office. The technician produced his equipment, a long steel rod with a small boxful of electronics attached to it at one end. He began making passes over the walls with it, at first with no result. 'Try the telephone,' said Wilberforce anxiously.

The technician unscrewed its base and found nothing. 'It's awkward fitting them into this model.' He went back to wielding his apparatus, which produced a bleep as he tested an area behind Celia's desk.

'Ah,' sighed Wilberforce, relieved.

The tiny microphone was behind a large framed photograph of a hybrid hellebore, Celia's pioneering cross between *corsicus* and *niger* which had laid the foundations of Archerscroft's prosperity. There was another microphone in the kneehole of the desk and two more in the outer office, one behind a filing cabinet and another under the flap of Monica's typing table.

145

'German,' commented the engineer. 'Most industrial spying equipment comes from there.'

'I wonder when they were installed,' said Wilberforce.

Celia remembered that the office had been burgled a few weeks ago. 'We thought it was teenagers after the petty cash, but I suppose we were wrong. Was the other end at the Tidmarshes'?'

'That's what we assume, certainly,' said Wilberforce.

She repressed a shudder at the thought that for weeks every word she uttered in the office had been overheard by the horrible Annabel, whom she had hated at first sight. To be eavesdropped on by Monica Porter was a different matter, she could be dismissed as a figure of fun. The only possible reaction to Annabel was disgust.

The engineer sealed up the microphones in an official envelope, against their use in evidence. When the office had been locked up, Wilberforce said: 'Now, Mrs Grant. My wife maintains that after what you've done for us, I owe you the most luxurious dinner that money can buy. Are you doing anything this evening?'

Appalled at the prospect of laborious conversation over a tête-à-tête dinner with a policeman with a one-track mind and an obsession with an unsolved case, she excused herself on the plea that she had urgent work to do, and invited him in for a quick drink to show that there was no ill feeling.

'So the Green Front is still on the rampage,' she began when she had settled him down with a whisky.

'Yes. There was another attack last night, in Lincolnshire.'

He seemed plunged in his own thoughts. Dinner, she decided, would have been a nightmare.

'Did the Tidmarshes tell you anything useful?' she asked.

He roused himself and told her the gist of what he had learnt from Edward. 'So what we've got is an innocent prank by some eco-enthusiasts which was taken over by a sinister figure with a Northern Ireland background, who enlarged it into a nation-wide terror campaign.'

He lapsed back into silence. Celia thought about what he had told her and came up with a question. 'The Tidmarshes knew all about these trails of treasure-hunt clues that led people to the arms caches, is that right?'

'Yes.'

'In that case, why did they have to be got out of the way while Annabel eavesdropped on me? If they knew, there was no reason why they shouldn't have stayed while she did it.'

'Yes,' said Wilberforce. 'It's an interesting thought, isn't it? Why did Hamilton have to get them out of the way?'

Next evening after closing time Bill and Celia worked late in the office, drafting Archerscroft's autumn catalogue. When they had finished Bill invited her to his cottage for 'bacon and eggs and a brew of tea'. Undeterred by the prospect of having to drink his overpoweringly strong tea, she accepted. The invitation meant that Jenny Watson's ghost no longer stood between them. They were back on their old relaxed and friendly footing.

After they had eaten they settled down in armchairs to a leisurely conversation broken by long silences. Though he had obviously got over Jenny, Celia did not mention her for fear of touching a nerve that might still be raw.

'Oh, I meant to tell you,' he said. 'While you was out lunch time, Mrs Fortescue rang. Wanted me to go up in the morning and give Hodson a hand, he'd got a bit behind.'

'You'll go? There's nothing special on tomorrow.'

'I thought I'd get them new little hostas potted on. I told her I was busy, so we'd send one of the girls, but she said no.'

Celia thought about this. Margaret Fortescue was a good customer. It would be a pity if she felt she was being cold-shouldered because her husband had run amok with a bulldozer and offended the village.

'Surely the girls can deal with those hostas?'

147

No reply.

The mood was right for late-night confidences. 'Bill, you don't like Mrs Fortescue, do you?'

'She's OK.'

'But that only means she doesn't make saucer eyes at you.'

'That's right.'

Suddenly she remembered. According to Mary Basset, Margaret Fortescue had a lover.

'But her husband's away a lot. Is there somebody, or doesn't she care for it?'

He thought for a moment. 'I dunno. She's never bothered me.'

'But you don't like her, Bill. Why not?'

There was a long pause. 'She's clever.'

'In what way?'

'She gets round you. She knows what you got on your mind and she manages so you tell her. She don't ask questions much, but somehow you tell her things you don't want to.'

'What sort of things?'

'Personal things.'

'Go on.'

'Like whether I got a girl and if not why not.'

'She asked you that and you told her?'

'Oh, yes, Celia. That's her cleverness. Before I knew where I was I'd told her about Anthea and the murder and all the dodgy things she did to me, things even you don't know, and how I didn't trust girls no more after that.'

'Bill, it's time you got over the Anthea business.'

His jaw tightened and a little muscle twitched in his cheek. 'I had, till that Jenny came along.'

'I know, the last thing you needed was a repeat dose of Anthea-style deceitfulness. I could cheerfully strangle Jenny. What else did Margaret ask you?'

'All about the nursery and how it worked.' A pause. 'And what I thought of you.'

Suddenly he was blushing scarlet, with thick veins standing out from his forehead below the thatch of very

148

blond hair. Horrors, she thought, he's dreadfully embarrassed, this is a black hole that I'm not going to explore. Then she realized: the rumour that he was her lover had probably reached Margaret, and she had asked him about it.

To slide away from the danger zone she said: 'Did Mrs Fortescue make you tell her what sort of girl you fancied?'

'It's not a case of fancying. It's what they're really like, what they got in their mind, and whether they're straight with you.'

'Nothing about blonde or dark, plump or thin? Tell me the full specification, in case I spot one that would do.'

'Oh Celia, get along with you. Don't you start that, you're as bad as Mrs Fortescue.'

Back at home, she was wide awake and unready for bed. For some days she had been working intermittently on a garden design: a commission from an architect who was building himself an ultra-modern house as a show-piece to attract clients and wanted a garden to match. The sketches she had been working on were still on her desk and she went back to them. Try as she might, her attempts to devise something suitable always ended up looking like the entrance courtyard of a public-relations firm. She went on juggling with paved and gravelled surfaces, raised beds, groupings of shrubs, and planters to be filled with bedding in season, but presently found that she was concentrating on quite a different problem.

Perhaps problem was the wrong word, it had not jelled into one yet. For the moment it was nothing more than a fantastic query, triggered off during her session with Bill. If there was anything in it, there would be a whole chain of queries leading one to another. If all the answers were right, it would turn everything that had happened over the past two months upside-down. But the answers were probably wrong.

It was worth putting it to the test, though. She would take the first step, which involved ringing Bill. It was very late, but no matter.

149

'Bill? I'm sorry if I've woken you up but I've been thinking and I need some information.'

'OK, Celia,' he said sleepily. 'Whassit about?'

'I'm going to repeat a question you refused to answer earlier, but it's important, I need to know. When Mrs Fortescue asked you what sort of girl you'd really go for, what did you tell her?'

'Oh, Celia, that's very personal.'

'Of course it is, but if you're prepared to talk about it to one of our customers, why can't you tell me? I wouldn't be asking without a good reason, so come on now. The specification for the future Mrs Wilkins.'

'There's no specification, and there won't be a Mrs Wilkins. I was put right off women again when that Jenny turned out to be such a rotten cow.'

'But Jenny hadn't burst on the scene till after Mrs Fortescue asked you for a specification, had she? I need to know what you told her. I'm sorry, but this really is important.'

'OK then Celia, I dunno why it's important, but if you say so I believe you, so here you are. The first thing was, she had to be clever, and kind with it. There's lots of clever unkind women and lots of dead boring kind ones. I said I'd go for a kind clever woman, that would keep me interested and not start rows.'

'What does "keeping you interested" mean?'

'Like having a good brain and telling me interesting things I don't know.'

'Fine, but what sort of things?'

'The history of famous people or about foreign countries, things I missed out on at school.'

'Poetry?'

'Yes! I learnt a poem by heart once because I liked it.'

'How old should she be?'

'Eighteen, nineteen. Quiet. I'd not want someone that had knocked around. If they're older, you have to reckon the lads have been at them, I wouldn't want anyone second-hand.'

'A shy virgin, in fact. Does it matter what she looks like?'

'It's fine if they're nice-looking, provided it's not turned

150

their head. I rather fancy a blonde, if she was fair the nippers would be too. I'd like that, having some kids that looked a bit like me.'

'That's terrific, Bill. Just what I wanted to know.'

'Is it? Celia, you're like a ferret at a rabbit-hole about this, why?'

'Because if you took the specification you gave to Mrs Fortescue and put it on the drawing board, you'd come up with a blueprint for inventing Jenny Watson.'

It took some time for this to sink in. 'Oh! Oh, yes, Celia, I see that. No, I don't see. What does it mean?'

'I've no idea, but I intend to find out.'

Wide awake and puzzled by her discovery, Celia was still in no mood for bed. She cleared her sketches for the architect's garden off her desk and sat staring at the blank expanse of leather. She could see the problem more clearly now, and started making a mental list of its key elements.

> The Tidmarshes had been kept out of their house, to prevent them knowing that Annabel Johnson was using it as a base from which to spy on Celia.
>
> Margaret Fortescue had made Bill provide her with a specification for his ideal girlfriend.
>
> Shortly afterwards, an actress purporting to correspond with the specification had appeared.
>
> Admiral Bond had complained of being spied on by Jason Fortescue, who had taken elaborate steps to punish him for offending his wife.
>
> Mrs Edgeley had made no secret of her opinion that Celia was a little goose, and not necessarily adorable.
>
> Jason Fortescue went in for lawsuits in a big way.

Having completed the list, she laid out each item in front of her mentally, as if they were cards in a game of patience that had to be solved. But the game would not come out. An essential card was missing. But suddenly she knew what the card was, and where it was to be found.

Next morning she rang Harry Winterbourne, an old

family friend who looked after her investments. 'Harry, I need to talk to you.'

'As always, Celia, I shall be delighted. What about?'

'A firm I'm interested in. One of those big international conglomerates, run by a man called Jason Fortescue.'

There was a pause. 'If you're wanting investment advice about that outfit, the answer is definitely no.'

'Actually that's not what I'm after.'

'Oh, dear, I suppose you're at it again, having yet another of your hair-raising and unladylike adventures? I wish you wouldn't.'

'I can't help it, it just happens.'

'How on earth did Jason Fortescue "happen" to you?'

'He lives just outside the village.'

'You mean, you're in contact with him personally?'

'Not really. But his wife's a customer of mine.'

'Oh, dear, some of the situations you stumble into make my blood run cold. Don't go anywhere near either of the Fortescues till we've talked. Can you come up to town? Today? How about lunch?'

Travelling up in the train, she was attacked by pangs of guilt, as she always was when she exploited Harry Winterbourne. Years ago, after his wife died, he had proposed to her. He was a very nice man, intelligent, eminent in his field, and extremely rich, but there was no question for her of a successor to Roger, and she had turned him down. He had not married anyone else, and it was an enormous tribute to his niceness that they were still friends.

They had arranged to meet at an old-fashioned chop house in the City. He greeted her with old-world courtesy to match the premises, but with an undertone of discreet amusement. 'You're incorrigible, Celia. You're seething with curiosity, too excited to eat. Let me order some food, though, and we'll talk while they're bringing it.'

He ordered, then said: 'Well? Where do I begin?'

'By telling me all about that lawsuit of Jason Fortescue's that the press made such a carry-on about a few years ago.'

'Ah. That's part of a much longer story, most of it steeped in iniquity.'

152

'What sort of iniquity? Cooking the books? Siphoning off money into private banks in Luxemburg? Rigging the market to support fraudulent takeover bids?'

'Nothing of the kind. From the financial point of view Hanbury-Fortescue Holdings is as clean as a whistle. Profitable, too.'

'Then why is it a fate worse than death as an investment?'

'Because it's a one-man show. Hanbury's dead. Everything depends on Fortescue. He runs a very tight ship, watches his subordinates like a hawk, makes all the policy decisions himself, even minor ones. If anything happened to him, the whole shooting match would collapse.'

'But why should anything happen to him?'

He looked at her severely over his glasses. 'Let me fill you in on a few facts about Fortescue. He was in the States when his partner, Gerald Hanbury, died in Australia. The verdict was suicide, but he was an uncomplicated cheerful sort of man and no one could imagine why he would want to kill himself. The managing director of one of Fortescue's Australian companies disagreed with him on policy and threatened to appeal to the shareholders over his head, but nothing came of it because of a sex scandal, rape of a minor, I think it was. It looked very like an entrapment, but he got five years. Fortescue sued a domestic appliances manufacturer for breach of contract and lost. It just happened that six months later there was a fire at the factory in which the managing director and three other people were killed. These things are never mentioned in the media because they know he'd come down on them at once with a libel action and escalate the costs till it ruined them, but everyone in the media and the City knows he's a man to steer clear of. He's totally devoid of any moral sense. If anyone gets in his way he behaves like a half-mad racketeer.'

'You can say that again,' Celia agreed, and told him about Baker's Meadow and Fortescue's savage revenge on the Admiral.

'Typical Fortescue behaviour,' Winterbourne commented. 'When anyone does him an injury he gets obsessive about it. That was what happened over the lawsuit. He spent a fortune on it, took it right up to the House of Lords.'

'I remember that vaguely. There were lots of headlines in the papers, but it was before the Fortescues came to live near Melbury, so I didn't take in the details. What was it all about?'

'Ah, I know the whole story, because one of our clients had a big holding in the firm he was sueing, some people called Frensham and Clark. He accused them of poaching one of his scientists who was doing research and development, a man called Arkwright. He said Arkwright had resigned and taken a job with Frensham and Clark, taking with him the results of years of research he had done for Hanbury-Fortescue. His case was that secret discoveries belonging to Hanbury-Fortescue had been handed over for further development and commercial exploitation to a rival firm.'

'Isn't it difficult to prove that sort of thing?'

'Very, and the whole affair was Fortescue's fault. It all started because he uses private enquiry agents to report on his senior employees' behaviour, and one of them unearthed the fact that this man Arkwright had a brother working for Imperial Chemical Industries, in other words for a competitor. Fortescue's the sort of man who sees conspiracies everywhere, so he flew into a rage and accused Arkwright of having committed a breach of trust by not reporting the relationship. Arkwright was taken off the sensitive research he was doing and given a stooge job in a backwater of the company, so he resigned and moved to Frensham and Clark.'

'Who did Fortescue sue? Arkwright, or the firm?'

'The first case was against Arkwright for breach of contract, but he lost on the ground that the way he'd treated Arkwright amounted to constructive dismissal. Then he went for the firm, that was the case he took right up to the Lords and lost. Paying his own costs and Frensham and Clark's set him back over three million.'

'Harry, what does Frensham and Clark make?'

154

'Chemicals, mostly. It was set up five years back with European Community money along with a lot of others in that depressed area round Liverpool, and they've done quite well. But Celia, what's all this about, I'm dying to know.'

By the time she had satisfied his curiosity, their food came. Having been brought up to believe that one should not talk business while one eats, she led the conversation into more general subjects. But half her mind was elsewhere, and as she finished her coffee she put one last question. 'Harry, what sort of chemicals do Frensham and Clark make?'

'I think agricultural, mostly.'

'Not horticultural?'

'I'm not sure. Does it matter?'

'Enormously, yes.' She gathered up her handbag and gloves. 'But I know where I can find out.'

'One moment before you go, Celia. I'm worried sick at the thought of you tangling with a man like Fortescue. Do be careful down in that crime-ridden village of yours.'

'I will, Harry. I must go now, thank you for a lovely lunch and for being so helpful.'

'Anything to oblige, Celia, you know that.'

At a payphone in the Mansion House Underground station, she rang the RHS laboratories at Wisley and put her question about Frensham and Clark to their expert on garden chemicals.

'They do make horticultural chemicals. I think their main outlet is in bulk supplies for use by commercial growers. But they also market their stuff under separate brand names for use by amateur gardeners, usually in diluted form for safety reasons.'

'Including things that make one's ecological hair stand on end?'

'One moment, I've got the list here. Yes. "Pestbane", their insecticide, is based on gamma HCH, which is an organochlorine and very persistent. "Slugdeath" contains methiocarb, which is even more toxic to birds than

155

methaldehyde, and "Fungaway" contains thiobendazole, which is broad-spectrum—'

'In other words, it's a pretty indiscriminate killer.'

'That's right. You use it to kill fungus. But it also kills fish and mites and worms, in fact it used to be used to cure tapeworms in animals and humans. It's also a mutagen, so if you're very fussy you accuse it of causing cancer. There are a lot more nasty things on the Frensham and Clark list, including something for keeping cats off flowerbeds that I don't like the look of at all.'

'In other words, the only eco-objectionable product they don't manufacture is peat.'

'That's right. Anything else you want to know?'

'No. That's fine. Thank you.'

'Glad to be of use.'

Celia knew at once what her next port of call had to be and plunged into the Underground, but with butterflies very active in her stomach. She was filled with her old dread of being laughed out of court by the police for telling an unbelievable story, and tried hard during the journey to marshal her ideas for presentation to Wilberforce. But her thoughts were still in turmoil when she found herself confronting the formidable glass slab of New Scotland Yard.

Nerving herself for the ordeal, she asked for Wilberforce at the reception desk and was told to wait, the implication being that as she had no appointment the wait would probably be a long one. In fact only a few minutes passed before he emerged from the lift and came loping towards her, wearing what in a man so severe-looking amounted to a radiant smile.

'Mrs Grant, how nice. What can we do for you?'

'Nothing, but . . . you know that man who has the machine that detects microphones? I think you should send him down to Melbury again, to search Admiral Bond's house and see if he can find any there.'

Nine

'I simply don't believe it,' said Wilberforce.

'It is a bit way out,' agreed Inspector Grigg.

'I don't believe it myself,' Celia confessed. 'It's just a wild idea that occurred to me because I couldn't think of any other explanation.'

They were in Wilberforce's office on the fourteenth floor of the Yard. Celia's halting explanation of her wild idea had left all three of them in a daze.

'There were all sorts of things that seemed to fit together,' she explained. 'When Marion Underhill turned up at Archerscroft, calling herself Jenny Watson and corresponding exactly to Bill Wilkins' specification, it was too much of a coincidence. Margaret Fortescue had extracted the specification from Bill, and I decided that she must be connected somehow with the Green Front. Then I remembered that her husband knew exactly when to intervene to frustrate Admiral Bond over Baker's Meadow. How? The Admiral's house is no further from the Tidmarshes' than mine, easily within range for Annabel Johnson's eavesdropping set up. That could be the explanation. Then I thought, Fortescue's behaving like a maniac towards the Admiral, he's obviously a man who never forgives even the smallest insult or injury. So I asked myself, what if there's someone else he hasn't forgiven, for instance that firm he brought a huge lawsuit against, and lost? Having got that far, I thought I'd better put a few questions to my stockbroker.'

There was a long pause. 'What we're trying to make ourselves believe,' Wilberforce summed up, 'is that

Fortescue decided to get even with a business competitor that he has an obsessive grudge against. But everyone knows that he has it in for Frensham and Clark, because he sued them and lost the case. He'll be the obvious suspect if their chemical plant is blown up or burnt down. So he invents the Fighters of the Green Front to do the job for him, claiming to do it for the purest ecological reasons. They take the blame and he's in the clear.'

'Yes,' said Celia unhappily. 'But it seems a very elaborate way of going about it.'

'Let's play around with it for a bit and see where it gets us,' Wilberforce suggested.

'Fortescue would have to do something to take the heat off himself,' Grigg argued. 'That is, if he's really capable of the sort of violence we're talking about.'

'My stockbroker thinks he is,' said Celia, 'judging from his record.'

'We could make some enquiries in the City,' Grigg suggested. 'Find out if other people agree.'

'Fortescue isn't taking much of a risk,' remarked Wilberforce. 'All the work and most of the planning is being done by this Northern Ireland character, Hamilton.'

'That's right,' said Grigg. 'The whole thing smacks of Hamilton's taste for complicated intrigue and black humour.'

'And unless a connection can be proved between him and Fortescue,' Celia added, 'no one can touch Fortescue, whatever they suspect. But how did Fortescue and Hamilton get together in the first place?'

'Good question,' said Wilberforce. 'If I knew the answer to that, I'd begin to take this way-out theory very seriously.'

After thinking for a moment Grigg reached for the phone. 'I've had an idea.'

'Fine. We need some,' commented Wilberforce.

'I'm ringing Colonel Timmins in Belfast,' Grigg explained. 'He says Hamilton did a contract job over there, killed the managing director of some firm. Who

158

put out the contract, I wonder? It's just a hunch of mine, I thought I'd ask Timmins who owned the firm.'

He put the query, was answered, and put down the phone. 'The majority shareholder was a man called Gerald Hanbury.'

'Who was Fortescue's partner and committed a not very convincing suicide in Australia,' Celia pointed out.

'And according to Timmins,' Grigg added, 'Hamilton went to Australia after they hoofed him out of Northern Ireland. Arranging a not very convincing suicide would be just his cup of tea.'

Wilberforce's eyebrows shot up. 'Well, well. We'd better think some more about this.'

There was a contemplative silence.

'As I see it the thing works out this way,' Wilberforce reasoned. 'Hamilton has done dirty work for Fortescue before. They put their heads together again because Fortescue wants to find a way of getting even with Frensham and Clark without making everyone point the finger at him. One or other of them suggests that Frensham and Clark are vulnerable from the green point of view. If an attack on them can be dressed up as a green outrage, it will put the blame firmly elsewhere. So Hamilton's told to nose around in green circles and see what he can come up with. Presently he stumbles on these innocents who plan a minor prank at the Chelsea Flower Show. He realizes that the thing has potential, sells the idea to Fortescue, blows up the Blandford fly scheme into a huge terrorist operation, and off we go.'

Grigg nodded. 'And Fortescue's happy. He's put up the money, apart from that his hands are clean.'

'It all fits together,' said Wilberforce, 'if you assume that Fortescue's mad.'

'Say you're a megalomaniac,' Celia argued, 'who's got away with several quite serious crimes committed for you by someone else. Don't you begin to think you can get away with anything, however fantastic?'

'Not with wide-awake ladies like you around, Mrs Grant,' said Wilberforce. 'If the Fortescues had had any sense they'd have tried the Jenny Watson trick on some-one else.'

'They don't know much about me. And what they do know comes from the Edgeleys, who are their only friends in the village. Grace Edgeley makes no secret of her belief that I'm a brainless goose with an inflated idea of my abilities as a Miss Marple.'

'How wrong can people be,' said Grigg with feeling.

'You wouldn't say that if you knew the atmosphere in the village,' replied Celia. 'After the crisis over Bill I tried to keep as quiet as possible about what I'd been up to, and a lot of interested parties circulated distorted versions of the truth. They're the people Grace Edgeley gets her information from.'

There was another long silence.

'Look, we've been beating about the bush long enough about this,' said Wilberforce. 'There's one simple way of finding out whether we're right or wrong. Are there, or are there not, microphones in Admiral Bond's house?'

'Yes, indeed,' Celia agreed. 'If there aren't any, I've been talking undiluted hot air.'

'We'll check on that at once,' said Wilberforce. 'And Grigg, take Foster with you and see what you can find out about Fortescue in the City. Someone had better go down to Melbury with Electronics, who, though – yes, Mrs Grant?'

She had looked shocked at the thought of a junior policeman confronting the Admiral in full flood of eccen-tricity. 'You couldn't possibly come yourself and impress the old gentleman? Admiral Bond's over eighty, he isn't exactly mad, but he's rather a handful and we don't want him spreading the glad news of his microphones all round the village.'

'No. If Fortescue knew they'd been discovered he'd lash out savagely in all directions, and he certainly mustn't be allowed to know that you've had a hand in exposing him. How do I keep the old gentleman quiet?'

'You don't mention the Green Front. You talk very mysteriously about a major security investigation of

160

nationwide importance, about which nothing can be said. The slightest leak would compromise the whole operation and you rely absolutely on his discretion. That might work, but I don't guarantee it.'

'Let's hope so. You're right, I ought to go to Melbury myself. It occurs to me that if you can wait a few minutes while I tie up the loose ends, I could give you a lift home.'

'Thank you, but my car's in the station car park at Welstead.'

'And of course you're anxious not to be seen with me in case you're compromised. At least let me organize a car to take you to your train.'

'No, really. That would be what they call wasting police time. Victoria Station's only at the end of the street. I shall take a bus.'

He looked worried. 'I suppose it's safe for you to travel on public transport. If Fortescue discovers your role in this affair, you'll be in very great danger.'

'It's fortunate, isn't it, that I insisted on being anonymous.'

'Very fortunate. Long may you continue to be so.'

'Nice place,' said Padstow, taking an eyeful of the Admiral's over-titivated Elizabethan house and cluttered garden.

Wilberforce's tug on the wrought iron bell-pull set up a distant clamour within. Presently the heavy oak door opened a few inches and the Admiral, in a cardigan and carpet slippers, peered out. Wilberforce identified himself and Padstow, but did not over-excite the old gentleman by mentioning the Special Branch.

'Scotland Yard, eh? And what can I do for you fellers?'

'What we'd like to talk to you about is very confidential,' said Wilberforce.

'Come in then, come in.'

He took them into the dark-panelled drawing room and hovered lovingly over the decanters. 'How about a spot? The sun's been over the yard-arm for hours. No? Later, perhaps. Sit down and tell me the story.'

161

Wilberforce stressed again that the matter was highly confidential. 'I hope you will keep what I'm going to tell you strictly to yourself.'

'Of course. Once a sailor, always a sailor. They used to call us the silent service. How can I help you?'

'We understand, sir, that someone has been spying on you, poking their nose into your private affairs.'

He frowned menacingly. 'Who told you that?'

'We have our sources.'

'Sorry. Keep the name to yourselves, I quite understand. You're right, though.'

'Am I right in thinking that you believe a man called Fortescue's behind it?'

'Filthy foreign bastard, that's not even his real name.' Bouncing in his chair with indignation, he unfolded the saga of Baker's Meadow, and the underhand way in which Fortescue had anticipated his every move. When this was over, Wilberforce said: 'Unfortunately, sir, you're not the only one who has suffered from his activities. Others have been spied on too.'

The Admiral's eyes opened wide. 'An espionage ring?'

'Industrial espionage, mainly. We're having to make enquiries in various parts of the country, in fact you could call this an investigation on a nationwide scale.'

'And this shocking feller Fortescue's at the bottom of it.'

'We think so, yes. And of course it's vital that he shouldn't get wind of our investigation till it's complete, and we're ready to make a number of arrests.'

'Ah. He has accomplices of course. In view of what happened to me, there must be one of them in the village. I had better give you a list of the possible suspects.'

'That won't be necessary, I hope. We think you've been under electronic surveillance. There's a technician outside in the car with equipment for detecting hidden microphones. With your permission I'd like him to check your house.'

The Admiral swelled visibly with self-importance. 'Electronic surveillance, eh? Let him come in, let him come in.'

162

The engineer found microphones in the living room and the dining room, as well as one attached to the telephone in the hall.

This was the moment when Wilberforce felt he was on firm ground at last. If Annabel Johnson had spied on the Admiral as well as on Mrs Grant, there was a direct link through her between Fortescue and the Green Front organized by Hamilton. Mrs Grant's way-out theory had received a powerful boost. Almost certainly, the aim of the operation was to punish Frensham and Clark for stealing his secrets and defeating him at law.

The Admiral too was delighted, as if the microphone somehow increased his status. 'We must celebrate this,' he crowed, homing in on the decanters. 'Superintendent, this is a single malt, you'll have a snort?'

Wilberforce would have liked to decline. But he sensed that the Admiral's own need was great, and that it would be considered a hostile act if they refused to keep him company. Besides, he was not quite sure he had said enough to make the confused old gentleman keep his mouth shut. A matey drinking session could be used to reinforce the message that Fortescue was a dangerous man who must on no account be allowed to realize that the net was closing round him. Sergeant Padstow, who was driving, was let off with orange squash, but the other two had to dispose of stupefying doses of single-malt whisky in the course of duty, while Wilberforce made one more attempt to ensure he did not endanger Mrs Grant by talking out of turn.

By mid-morning next day Grigg and Foster were ready to report on what they had discovered from contacts in the City, back files of newspapers, and a journalist specializing in agricultural affairs. Hanbury's suicide in Australia bore all the hallmarks of a Hamilton operation, including a distressed phone call of Hanbury's to a colleague, in which he had spoken in a voice 'barely recognizable through agitation' of his intention to kill himself. The same applied to the sex scandal which had put an end to the career of the manager of a Hanbury-Fortescue

163

plant in the outskirts of Sydney. The defence plea alleging an entrapment had been rejected by the jury, but only by a majority verdict. Newspaper accounts of Fortescue's massive lawsuit showed that the bone of contention had been Dr Arkwright's work on the development of a new agricultural fertilizer which was cheaper and more effective than nitrate. He had completed the project after his transfer to Frensham and Clark, and the firm had almost finished constructing a plant at its Merseyside factory which was to manufacture the product on a commercial scale. Meanwhile, work along the same lines had continued, though more slowly, in the Hanbury-Fortescue camp, and their production plant was almost half built. 'So if Fortescue blew up the Frensham and Clark plant,' Grigg reported, 'he could collar the market while they were still rebuilding.'

'You say this fertilizer is cheaper and more efficient than nitrate,' said Wilberforce. 'Is it more eco-friendly?'

'That seems to be a matter of opinion. It doesn't run off into rivers like nitrate and pollute them, and the Ministry of Agriculture has passed it. But something similar has failed its tests in the States and there are fairly loud murmurs here from the quarters you'd expect about mutagenic effects and cancer.'

'In other words, Frensham and Clark is a credible Green Front target, and the sooner we get on to them the better.'

Within the hour Wilberforce, Padstow, Grigg, and Forster were speeding north on the motorway. As they circled round Birmingham, it occurred to Wilberforce to ask: 'Do we know if this Dr Arkwright is still on their payroll?'

'My sources think not,' said Grigg. 'They believe he's in the States.'

'Good, that's one worry out of the way. Given half a chance, Fortescue would blow him up along with the plant.'

Presently they were threading through a depressed area of Lancashire, where unemployment was high and abandoned cotton mills and empty engineering works lined the road on either side. In the midst of this dereliction, the Frensham and Clark production plant shone like a good and prosperous deed in a naughty and poverty-stricken world. There was fresh paint, an air of bustle, and a lot of shining new pipework with men working on it. Wilberforce was pleased to see that security was strict. Though he had given advance notice of his visit, he was made to show his credentials at the gate before the car was allowed through.

Bernard Smithson, the managing director, was waiting for them in a no-frills office in which no money had been spent on impressive furniture or public-relations house plants. He wasted no time in getting down to business.

'It's good of you to come all this way to warn us that Fortescue's on the warpath again, but we knew that already. Security here is very strict, and Arkwright's got round-the-clock protection.'

'He's in the States, we understand.'

'No, that's what the switchboard's told to say when people ask for him. He's working at home five miles away with a computer terminal and fax machine and a twenty-four-hour bodyguard.'

'We have reason to believe,' said Wilberforce, 'that there may be an attempt very shortly to attack your plant.'

Smithson looked surprised. 'Oh, surely. Fortescue wouldn't be mad enough to attempt that, everyone would know he was behind it.'

'As far as the public's concerned, it wouldn't be him doing the attacking. The plant would have been blown up for the best possible environmental motives by these people who call themselves the Green Front. They'd say they'd done it because they disapprove of some of the chemicals you manufacture.'

'What? Those half-mad people?'

'Yes. They're financed and masterminded by Fortescue.'

Smithson thought for a moment. 'This is a very nasty

165

scenario. They could do us a lot of damage. We've almost finished building a new plant to manufacture the stuff that he accuses us of stealing from him, a fertilizer that solves the problem of run-off into rivers that you get with nitrate. If the Green Front wrecked our plant before it went on-stream, Fortescue would get in first and collar the market, which is worldwide and huge. But it's so bare-faced, would he really dare?'

'Your guess is as good as mine, but let's assume for a moment that he's going to. Does he have a spy in the plant?'

'I assume so, Superintendent. I am aware of the facts of life.'

'Could the spy smuggle a bomb in?'

'A little one, yes. But the people on the gate keep a sharp lookout. I like to think he couldn't get a big enough one in to do real damage.'

'Then the obvious danger is a car bomb. Is there anywhere outside the perimeter fence where they could get one near enough to the new plant to do serious damage?'

'Not really, nothing we couldn't repair.'

'Then they've got to get the vehicle in.'

'The gates are reinforced steel. We lock them at night.'

'Good. Can we have a look round, see if anything occurs to us?'

They toured the half-built plant, noting where the vulnerable areas were in relation to points where deliveries might be made, such as the canteen and the store for construction materials. 'If I was Fortescue,' Wilberforce suggested, 'I'd hi-jack a vehicle from one of your suppliers, load a bomb on to it, and get it past the gatekeeper.'

'So we put extra security men on the gate,' said Smithson.

'Armed police marksmen,' Wilberforce corrected. 'But that's not enough. People live round here. I don't like the thought of an armed bomb with a timing device held up in your gateway.'

'What more can you do?' Smithson asked.

166

'Intercept the attack before it gets here.'

'Fine, but how?'

'There are ways. It's easier if you know roughly when the attack's going to happen.'

'I can tell you exactly,' said Smithson. 'Or rather, I can make an inspired guess. It will happen the day after tomorrow.'

'Fine, but why?'

'Arkwright works at home, right? Fortescue would dearly love to kill him, he's had someone sniffing around his place lately, sussing out the bodyguards and so on. Now, Arkwright will be here on Thursday morning to look at progress on the construction site. How about Fortescue killing two birds with one stone?'

'It's possible. But could Fortescue's spy have found out that he's coming?'

'It's a regular date, every other Thursday.'

Wilberforce's eyebrows shot up in disapproval. Regular dates meant bad security.

'I know, but we can't help it,' said Smithson. 'It's the only day the consulting engineer can manage, and Arkwright never comes by the same route. Shall we put him off?'

Wilberforce thought for a moment. 'No. Let him come. I'll buy this hunch. We'll set a trap, and he can be the bait.'

Over by Wilberforce's car, Padstow was making urgent signals.

'It looks to me as if you're wanted,' said Smithson.

Padstow was brandishing the carphone. Wilberforce hurried across to take the call, which was from the Yard. A bomb had just gone off at the Consolidated Chemicals plant near Northwich, causing extensive damage but no casualties. Wilberforce passed the news on to Smithson.

'This doesn't alter my reading of the situation. They attack other people, hoping to get the attack on you lost in the crowd.'

Smithson looked startled. 'You know who that firm belongs to, Superintendent? Fortescue.'

167

Wilberforce's mind reeled. For a moment, the carefully built up case against Fortescue seemed to be collapsing. 'Would he really do that? Score an own goal against himself to establish that he's not behind the attack on his enemy and competitor?'

'On second thoughts,' Smithson decided, 'I don't think it is an own goal. That plant makes pentachlorophenol, which is a pretty nasty fungicide; lethal to fish and cats, and suspected of causing birth defects and interfering with the immune system. Sooner or later the government's going to ban it.'

'So Fortescue gets his plant for making it blown up and collects the insurance, instead of having to close it down and write it off.'

'That's my guess. You'll be off there to find out what's what, I imagine. Give me a buzz if I'm right, I'll be interested.'

Northwich was only forty miles away, and Padstow covered the distance in half an hour flat. According to the Anti-Terrorist incident officer on the site, the attack on the plant had been mounted with considerable skill. A van belonging to a caterer which supplied the firm's canteen had been hi-jacked. A bomb had been loaded into it, and the hi-jacker, who had taken the place of the regular driver, had not been challenged at the gate. A confederate had then telephoned a twenty-minute warning to clear the site, the bomber had walked out unnoticed among the work-force, and the bomb had duly gone off. It had clearly contained massive quantities of explosive, probably home-made. The police were still looking for fragments of the timer. Even if he had been on the spot in time, the bomb expert would have been unable to defuse it during the warning period, because it would undoubtedly have been booby trapped.

The Green Front's intelligence had been good. Thanks to accurate information, presumably supplied to it by Fortescue, it had planted the car-bomb in a position where it would do maximum damage to the firm's capacity for making pentachlorophenol. When the Front rang to claim responsibility afterwards, it explained that this was exactly the aspect of the firm's operations that it intended to attack. It also announced that its operations had entered a new phase. Its activities so far had consisted only of trifling gestures intended to draw public attention to the danger posed by noxious horticultural chemicals. The serious work of attacking plants manufacturing them would now begin. Without knowing it, they had given notice that the attack on Frensham and Clark was imminent.

Wilberforce phoned Smithson with the news. 'It confirms our hunch about Thursday, doesn't it? Gives us nice time to get organized.'

For the next forty-eight hours he was hectically busy, but by the Wednesday evening he was ready to address a briefing session for detectives from all over the northwest of England. 'We're assuming that the attack will take place at or shortly after eleven a.m. tomorrow, when a man who is one of the bomber's targets will arrive at the plant. Though there are other possibilities, I propose to assume that the method will be the same as at Northwich, or a variant of it, and that a vehicle will be hi-jacked for use as a car-bomb. I have a list here of all the firms which make deliveries to Frensham and Clark, and we have checked that only three of them intend making a delivery tomorrow. In all three cases the regular driver is being asked to hand over to one of you. Two unmarked police cars will be detailed to shadow each of them, but of course they will not attempt to prevent the hi-jack, because we want to find the bomb as well as the bomber. The hi-jacked vehicle is to be followed discreetly and arrests made only when it is clear that the bomb is about to be put on board. To make this part of the operation easier a small radio beacon will have been fitted to the three vehicles which are liable to be hi-jacked.

'It is of course possible that some other method of delivering the bomb will be used, or that a vehicle not under our surveillance will arrive at the gates of the plant. A bomb-disposal officer will be in attendance there, but the situation will be extremely dangerous because the bomb will probably be booby-trapped. In addition to the bomb-disposal officer, two men per shift have been detailed to double up with the firm's security guards on the factory gate, and six armed police marksmen will be out of sight immediately inside it. My command post and communications centre will be in a disused warehouse opposite the gate of the plant, and I shall have six uniformed constables with me, to clear the area if it becomes necessary.

'The next step is to assign duties to individuals. But first, are there any questions?'

Looking back on the case after it was over, Wilberforce remembered the period after the break-up of the briefing session as an abysmally dark hour before the dawn. When he was not agonizing over the prospect of large-scale carnage, he was tormenting himself with the thought that his whole chain of reasoning was probably faulty; that rumour had exaggerated Fortescue's capacity for evil; that the next attack would be elsewhere, so that he had caused a great many policemen to mount a fruitless vigil.

The three vehicles due to make deliveries at the plant were a low-loader bringing concrete castings and reinforcing rods for the new plant, a truck containing pumping gear, and a van which supplied the plant's washrooms with roller towels. The driver of the low-loader had refused flatly to hand over his vehicle to a detective with no licence to drive a vehicle that size, but the others complied. Followed by unmarked police cars all three set off to deliver their burdens to Frensham and Clark.

The van containing roller towels set off just after ten. Presently one of the police teams following it reported that it had been boxed in by two cars and stopped. In accordance with their instructions both the shadowing cars drove past it without appearing to take notice, and followed it with the aid of its radio beacon. But to Wilberforce's alarm it did not divert into a hide-out to load the bomb, but continued its normal route. In answer to urgent enquiries from Wilberforce, one of the squad cars reported that there was only one person on board, the driver. 'We think it's a girl.'

'What d'you mean, you think so?'

'Jeans and a T-shirt. But we're pretty sure we saw a pair of knockers.'

'Blonde, was she?'

'No. Dark, with a pony tail.'

'What happened to the other hi-jackers?'

'We got their car numbers.'

But in accordance with their instructions, they did nothing that might warn the hi-jackers that the bomber was driving into a trap.

She had still not diverted from her route to pick up the bomb. When she was within five minutes of the factory gate, Wilberforce woke up to the truth. 'This is the get-away car. It delivers its load, sits around till the vehicle with the bomb in it is in place, and drives out with the bomber as a passenger.'

But where was the vehicle with the bomb in it? There was no report of another hi-jack.

Promptly at eleven a carful of bodyguards, with the small figure of Dr Arkwright sandwiched between them, drove into the plant. The trap was set, but there was still no sign of a bomb.

But as Wilberforce waited tensely, a dark-blue Vaux-hall appeared, driven by a man in a construction worker's hard hat. It advanced at a dignified pace and turned in at the gate. The watchers in the warehouse stiffened into attention.

'Who's this?' Grigg murmured.

'Didn't you see?' said Wilberforce. 'It was Hamilton.'

Across the road the two men on the gate approached the car. Hamilton produced an identity card with a photo-graph. 'Health and Safety Executive. I've come to make a snap inspection of safety on your construction site.'

'Thank you, sir. There is a practice security alert on this morning, but we won't keep you a moment.'

While one of them checked the interior of the car, the

other inspected its underside with the help of a mirror mounted at an angle on the end of a long rod.

'Thank you, sir. And now would you mind opening the boot?'

'Oh, I don't think that will be necessary. I'm all for firms practising security, but after all I am a government official.'

'I'm sorry, sir. I have orders to insist.'

After a moment in shock, Hamilton engaged reverse and began to back out of the entrance and make a dash for freedom. But the bomb-disposal officer was beside the driver's door. 'I shouldn't do that unless you want to set the bomb off.'

Hamilton turned and saw that he was about to ram an unmarked police car which had moved in behind him, blocking his escape. 'We'll all be blown up if you open the boot,' he said calmly. 'It's booby-trapped.'

'Have we time to get the work-force out?'

'Fifteen minutes. You'll have to hurry.'

Uniformed police from the disused warehouse began clearing the neighbouring streets. The factory siren brayed a warning, and the workers in the plant began streaming out of the gate, eyeing Hamilton's car nervously as they passed it.

Sandwiched among a group of women from the canteen was the driver of the hi-jacked van, a girl with a head scarf over dark hair arranged in a pony tail. As she passed Hamilton she threw him a despairing glance. Wilberforce and his men were far too preoccupied to notice her as she passed by in the crowd, let alone to realize that they were letting Marion Underhill, alias Jenny Watson, walk past them to freedom disguised in a dark wig.

The two security men had handcuffed Hamilton to the steering-wheel, then left the bomb-disposal officer to deal with him.

'Now,' said the bomb-disposal man, 'how do I defuse the booby-trap?'

'I will tell you when I have been released and removed to a safe distance.'

'No way. You'd lie to me, let me blow myself up, and hope to escape in the confusion. You're going to tell me now.'

Hamilton grinned savagely. 'I don't think I shall, we must both take our chance. Let's see how clever you are. Incidentally, we know each other, don't we? From Northern Ireland.'

'Possibly, but don't let's waste time. How long have we got?'

With an awkward movement, Hamilton consulted his wristwatch. 'About eleven minutes.'

The officer began speaking into his microphone, a routine precaution when defusing a bomb. Should anything go wrong, he would not survive to tell the tale. To make it possible for his successors to benefit from his experience, he described every move he intended to make before he made it.

'I shall now defuse the booby-trap, which is probably activated by the lock of the boot, which I shall leave severely alone. The car is a hatchback, so I shall release the catch securing the back of the rear seat and pull it forward so that I can look into the boot. If our bomber values his skin as much as I do mine, he will speak up before I do anything disastrous.'

'I'm not saying anything,' growled Hamilton.

'I have now released the seat and am looking into the boot. It contains a cardboard box about four feet by three by two high. I can see no detonator, but the glass cover and bulb of the boot light have been removed and a wire issuing from the socket disappears to the rear of the cardboard box. Opening the boot would make the light come on and activate the booby trap. Unless otherwise advised by our bomber I shall cut this wire.'

'You have eight minutes left,' said Hamilton.

'I shall now unlock the boot . . . Ah yes. The timing device is an ordinary P34, but there is one unusual feature, a wire running from the timer which by-passes the battery and disappears into the right-hand rear-light assembly of the car.'

173

'Do stop chattering and get on with it,' growled Hamilton. 'You have only five minutes left.'

'I am now testing this wire. It is not live, but I see now why it is there. The bulbs have been removed from the rear lights on both sides, and I assume that the sidelight bulbs in front have also been removeu. The intention is that the timer should be activated by moving the lighting switch to the sidelight position. As the wire is dead, I assume that the bomber wisely refrained from arming his bomb till he had finished jolting it around the countryside and deposited it safely in the position where it was to be detonated.'

'Two minutes left,' intoned Hamilton.

'On the contrary, I have all the time in the world. The sidelights have not been switched on and there is no danger. I shall cut the wire as an extra precaution, but I assume that this portentous count-down is our bomber's idea of a joke.'

'Well, I thought I might as well make you sweat a bit,' said Hamilton, grinning savagely.

Ten

Wilberforce came out of Hamilton's cell at the Scrubbs, convinced that he had been wasting his time. For three days Hamilton had sat staring at the wall while questions were fired at him by relays of interrogators, and had given no sign that he had even heard what he was being asked. It was the standard IRA technique for resisting interrogation, taught to every recruit on his indoctrination course.

Yet Wilberforce had to persist. He had no case against Fortescue unless he could break Hamilton down and make him talk. Only two other members of the Green Front were behind bars: two young men who had been involved in the hi-jack of the van full of roller towels. They were both brainless yobbos with a record of violent crime, and had been caught trying to sell one of the getaway cars used in the hi-jack; a foolish undertaking, since the police had circulated its description and registration number. Under intensive questioning they proved to know only what Hamilton had told them, namely that the Front was being financed by a half-mad millionaire who had the environment on the brain.

'And we wouldn't be any better off if we caught any of the others,' Wilberforce grumbled. 'Hamilton will have told them exactly the same thing.'

'What about his girlfriend, Marion Underhill?' said Grigg. 'She might be in the know.'

'Yes, but where is she?'

'God knows. Was it her disguised in a wig that drove the roller-towel van?'

175

'Could be. Damn this thing, John. We're in a proper fix.'

In a dingy room in run-down Liverpool, Marion Underhill lay on the bed she had shared with Hamilton, thinking. She refused to let herself sink into despair at the failure of the attack on the Frensham and Clark plant. She had always been a fighter, and the fight would go on.

She had been protesting all her life; at schools which lost patience with her one after another and expelled her; at the Academy of Dramatic Art which had cast her incongruously as Lady Windermere with a bustle and an outsize fan; in various animal welfare movements which had been horrified by her pleas for direct action. Her prison sentence had toughened her. The arrest of her lover and environmental guru was a severe blow, but the fight for a chemical-free horticulture must go on, Michael in his prison would expect it of her. She knew she had a first-class brain and she intended to use it. With the help of others who had been close to him, she began to pick up the threads of the campaign.

But one of the problems was finance. Unfortunately there were not very many environmentally aware people who were prepared to contemplate direct action, and Michael had relied far too heavily in her opinion on yobbos who were in it for the money. They had to be paid. But Michael, who was a secretive man, had not told her the name of the eccentric millionaire whose open purse and enthusiasm for green causes had made the campaign possible. Fortunately she had one or two clues, including a strong suspicion that the millionaire had lived somewhere near Melbury in Surrey. Michael had a contact there whom he visited regularly, but in great secrecy, almost always late at night. She also had a small notebook containing contact telephone numbers, which he had wisely left behind when going into action at Frensham and Clark's. He had disguised the numbers with a simple subtraction code, but she had watched him pencilling in the figures of the key underneath the coded numbers and knew how to decode them. They had already yielded

176

useful information on the whereabouts of explosives caches and safe houses. Why should they not also yield the contact number of the mysterious millionaire?

Rousing herself, she went to the local public library, found the telephone directory for the Reigate area, and settled down to do some serious research.

Returning in gloomy mood from his unprofitable session at Wormwood Scrubbs, Wilberforce remembered that he ought to ring Celia and congratulate her on being right about Fortescue's designs on Frensham and Clark.

'You're the one to be congratulated,' she replied.

'Not really, I don't consider it a success. Fortescue's the real villain behind all this, but he's going to get off scot-free. We haven't a shred of evidence against him.'

'Hamilton is shielding him, is that it?'

'That's right. He's obviously agreed to keep quiet in exchange for several million pounds, to be paid him when he comes out of prison. Unfortunately, he's our only chance of getting anything on Fortescue.'

'Aren't there accomplices who'll talk?'

'The others have all been told a cover story about a millionaire obsessed with the environment. He's supposed to be financing the Front.'

'But there's one exception, isn't there,' Celia suggested. 'Annabel Johnson. She must be in the know, she reported direct to Fortescue on Admiral Bond's attempt to buy Baker's Meadow. You might get at him through her.'

'We might if we could trace her, but we can't. We thought she might be one of the women employees at the Hanbury-Fortescue headquarters in London, but none of them correspond to your description of Annabel. I suppose she could be some kind of mistress of his, but it seems unlikely if she's as unattractive as you say.'

'Actually, Superintendent, I've had a vague idea about that.'

'Do please go on. I have a high opinion of your vague ideas.'

'I've been thinking about Annabel. I don't usually have

a strong reaction about the attractiveness or otherwise of women, and I wondered why she repelled me so. The other day it occurred to me that I'd get quite severe gooseflesh if she was a man dressed up.'

'Ah. D'you really think that's a possibility?'

'Yes. I do. With that sort of wispy fair hair and pasty face, you wouldn't notice the difference if he was careful how he shaved. And the feminine mannerisms were all rather awkward, as if they were an act.'

'If you're right, Mrs Grant, it would account for something else that puzzled me. Why did she leave her prints all over the Tidmarshes' cottage? Answer, because wearing gloves all the time would have been a nuisance, and the risk wasn't very serious if no one was going to be looking for the fingerprints of a man.'

'Or try to match the woman's description with a man on Fortescue's staff.'

'Mrs Grant, this is the third time you've pointed me in a promising direction when I didn't know which way to turn. Thank you. I shall follow this up at once.'

He followed it up by organizing a burglary at the headquarters of the Hanbury-Fortescue commercial empire, which was housed in an elegant late-Georgian house in Curzon Street. When the staff arrived for work next morning, they were displeased but not surprised to find that a first-floor window at the back had been broken and two expensive computers were missing. They reported the loss to the police because a condition of the firm's insurance policy required them to do so. No one expected the police to do anything about such a minor everyday occurrence.

But to everyone's surprise, a detective sergeant and two constables arrived within the hour, and asked to take everyone's fingerprints; for elimination, they explained. Prints belonging to members of staff would be destroyed as soon as any not accounted for had been identified. Presumably they would be those of the burglar.

This caused even greater surprise, since everyone knew

that even the most naïve teenage criminals took the precaution of wearing gloves. With a cynical disregard for the truth, the detectives replied that a member of the public had given a detailed description of a man not wearing gloves whom he had seen late at night walking away from the back of the premises and carrying what looked like a computer. They claimed to have recognized the description and said they had hopes of making an arrest. As the suspect had not worn gloves while removing his booty, there was a faint possibility that he might have left prints in the building, and it would be much easier to get a conviction if fingerprint evidence could be produced.

After making a not very thorough search for fingerprints in areas thought to have been visited by the burglar, the police withdrew. To avoid arousing suspicion, Wilberforce decided to hang on to the two computers for a month before 'recovering' them from the member of the Special Branch who had been detailed to steal them, and returning them to the firm.

This operation produced a surprising and satisfactory result, but a shadow was cast over Wilberforce's euphoria by a call from Mrs Grant. 'I'm sorry to bother you, Superintendent, but I'm a bit worried about Admiral Bond.'

'Oh dear. Indiscretions?'

'Only vague ones, fortunately. Dark hints about high-level intelligence matters that he's not in a position to disclose, at least not yet.'

'He hasn't actually mentioned Fortescue?'

'No, only that certain people are going to get their come-uppance. But that's bad enough, everyone knows who he means. I shall start trembling in my shoes if Fortescue gets to hear about that.'

'You're safe for the moment. He's in the States, distancing himself from the goings-on at Frensham and Clark's.'

'He may be, but his wife isn't. She's involved, she briefed Hamilton with the specification for "Jenny Watson".'

179

'This is very disturbing, we can't have you endangered. I'll call on Admiral Bond tomorrow and try to make him pipe down.'

The Admiral greeted him with renewed offers of whisky and asked how the case against 'that rotter Fortescue' was progressing.

'It's proving even more complicated than we thought,' Wilberforce replied. 'I'm afraid you can't expect results for some months, perhaps even a year. Meanwhile, secrecy is vital.'

'I am as silent as the grave, Superintendent.'

'Perhaps, but it's important not to throw out hints, however vague, that something is afoot. I am informed that you have done so several times.'

'Nonsense. Who says?'

'We have our sources.'

'Oh, really, Superintendent. A man as prominent in village affairs as I am is bound to make enemies. You mustn't listen to malicious gossip.'

'I always try not to, but I must stress again that any leak could have very serious consequences. May I have your assurance that you will avoid saying anything that might cause one?'

'I gave you that assurance when you came here before. There is no need to renew it.'

With this, Wilberforce had to be content.

His next call was at the Red Lion, in a village on the far side of Welstead, where he had arranged to meet Mrs Grant.

'You look as if you have news for me,' he said as she came in.

'I have, but let's hear yours first.'

He produced a photograph of a plumpish fair-haired man coming out of the Hanbury-Fortescue headquarters building in Curzon Street. 'Is that Annabel?'

'I think so. Yes, I'm sure it is.'

'Good. His fingerprints fit with the ones in the Tidmarshes' cottage.'

'But who is he?'

'His name's John Horton. He's the driver of the head-quarters Rolls-Royce. But he seems to spend most of his time sitting about in the outer office at Curzon Street, because he's Fortescue's spy there.'

'Really?' said Celia. 'Like those KGB colonels who used to dress up as chauffeurs and spy on the Eastern bloc ambassadors they drove about? How did you find that out?'

'We put a tap on Horton's home phone. He rang Fortescue last night in New York. Nothing sensational, just a routine report on who went where in the car, and who called at the office. Incidentally, Fortescue's coming home. Horton's meeting him at Heathrow on Friday.' He sighed, and fixed his sad, drooping eyes on Celia. 'There isn't enough evidence. I've a horrid feeling that Fortescue's going to get off scot-free as usual.'

'Connecting the two of them over the Annabel carry-on isn't enough?'

'Not really, a jury would get very confused. We need a cast-iron case and frankly I'm not hopeful.'

'But Fortescue must be brought to trial,' said Celia.

Concern for law and order was not her only consider-ation. In the long term, Fortescue was liable to prove an awkward neighbour. Sooner or later, he was sure to find out how deeply she had been involved with the police, and he had had worldwide experience in the art of getting away with murder.

'Yes,' Wilberforce sighed. 'There's your safety to con-sider.' He described his unsatisfactory interview with Admiral Bond, then added: 'If he doesn't keep quiet, your position in the village might become untenable.'

'I think it already has, more or less. My news is small beer compared with yours, but you'd better hear it. The Fortescues are giving a lunch party on Sunday, and I've been invited. His wife says he wants to meet me and congratulate me on my tasteful contribution to the design of their garden.'

'Mrs Grant, you *haven't* accepted?'

'Of course I have. I couldn't have refused without

making them suspect that I knew why I'd been asked and wanted to chicken out. They've invited another local couple, so there can't be any druggings or beatings up. I shall have to tell a lot of lies, but I'm quite good at that.'

'I'm worried. We ought to arrange some protection for you.'

'Policemen rushing out from behind the curtains at the crucial moment, brandishing handcuffs? No, really, I'll be quite all right.'

Wilberforce went on voicing his worries, but soon saw that she had stopped listening. Her mouth was open, and she was staring dazedly into vacancy.

'Mrs Grant, is anything wrong?'

She came back slowly to reality. 'No. But I've just had what I think is rather a good idea.'

When she had explained, he said: 'It's not "rather good", it's a stroke of genius, it's almost sure to give us the evidence we want. But it's risky. Would you really?'

'Look, I'm not a very brave person. But I don't want to spend years wondering what Fortescue's going to find out, and what he'll do to me when he does. I'd rather take a bit of a risk now to get rid of him.'

He looked at her earnestly. 'Do you really mean that?'

'Of course. Let's get down to detail and work out a plan of campaign.'

But by the Sunday morning she was regretting this macho attitude and had to fight down the butterflies in her stomach as she prepared for the party. What to wear had been an enormous problem. Before letting her go anywhere near the Fortescues, Wilberforce had insisted on equipping her with a panic button, similar to the ones issued to old people living alone, so that they could summon help if they had a fall. She was supposed to hang it round her neck on a string, and press it if the going got rough. But most of the dresses she tried on proved too close-fitting, so that the panic button was outlined beneath them in a tell-tale bulge which made her look deformed. The only exception was a very overpowering printed silk outfit with a draped front, which had survived

182

from the grand days of her marriage. She arrayed herself in it, hung the panic button round her neck, and set off for Kenlake.

Mastering her nerves, she turned into the rhododendron avenue inside Kenlake's entrance gate and headed across the open parkland beyond. Grigg and Foster, detailed to keep watch and answer the panic button if necessary, were lying in wait in the woods overlooking the park, and the knowledge that they were there helped to steady her as she drew up in front of the house.

The door was opened by a thug disguised as a butler; a giant with a boxer's broken nose whom she recognized as one of the bodyguards who went everywhere with Fortescue. She had presented herself a polite five minutes after the time she had been invited for. But she was the first guest to arrive, and was attacked at once by an extra worry she had not expected. Instead of being shown into a grand drawing room, she was ushered by the ex-boxer into a sitting room littered with Sunday papers, compact discs, and books, where she was greeted by Margaret Fortescue in slacks and a blouse, and her husband in an open-necked shirt. This was not to be a formal lunch. She was absurdly overdressed.

Fortescue stepped in at once to put her at her ease. 'What a vision of youth and beauty! How do you do it, not by living on lettuce leaves, I hope?'

'On the contrary, Mr Fortescue. I eat like a horse.'

'Do call me Jason, please. Now before the others come I want to walk you round the garden and tell you how much I admire what you've done. We invited you early on purpose.'

His comments as they made the tour were those of an intelligent layman who respected someone else's speciality. He seemed a different person from the grim bully who had confronted Admiral Bond in Baker's Meadow. Like many wicked people, he had charm.

As they returned to the house the Edgeleys arrived. Celia was pleased to see them, and not only because they too were overdressed for the occasion. Grace Edgeley's

183

firm belief that she was irredeemably stupid was exactly the view of herself that Celia wished to impress on the Fortescues.

Jason Fortescue began pouring drinks. Grace Edgeley said 'Wilfrid!' sharply to remind him, unnecessarily, that it was his job to distribute them. Celia asked for a white wine and soda water spritzer, on the plea that she would be driving. But she also needed to navigate her way through the perils of lunch with a clear head.

The first assault, which came soon after they sat down, was on the subject of the Admiral. 'How is he?' Margaret Fortescue asked. 'We feel rather bad about him.'

'We do indeed,' her husband chimed in. 'I was terribly sorry about that awful scene, but Baker's Meadow was ripe for development and the village needs more houses.'

'He brought it on himself,' said Grace Edgeley, looking reproachfully at Celia, 'aided and abetted by people who should have known better.'

'Celia, you're quite friendly with him,' said Margaret. 'Has he forgiven us at all?'

'Not entirely, I'm afraid.'

Fortescue paused with his fork in midair. 'Someone told me, I think it was you, Wilfrid, that he'd been sounding off mysteriously about a high-level spy scandal in the village. What on earth does he mean?'

'Goodness knows,' Wilfrid answered, 'but he says certain people are going to get their come-uppance.'

'I suppose that means me.'

'I shouldn't worry too much about it,' Celia observed mildly. 'Admiral Bond told me once that he'd worked in Naval Intelligence for a time, and at his age you tend to live in the past. He's probably got spies on the brain.'

'He's senile,' said Grace, 'mad as a hatter. Wilfrid quite likes him but I can't think why.'

Sounding very casual, Fortescue said: 'I wonder if Bond really thinks I'm spying on him?'

'He hasn't said anything like that to me,' Celia lied. 'But he does suffer a bit from delusions and I suppose it would be natural for him to cast you as the villain of the piece.'

'You don't think he's got any nasty little surprises up his sleeve.'

Celia opened wide innocent eyes. 'Good gracious no, what could he have?'

Fortescue let the subject drop, and Margaret started a general conversation which lasted almost to the end of the meal. Celia took little part. She was nerving herself against the time when she would have to deliver her bombshell.

Presently the talk degenerated into village gossip, from which Margaret's question arose quite naturally. 'By the way, Celia, what happened about that nice girl who was working for you, the one who disappeared?'

'The one who had an affair with your head gardener,' crowed Grace, in the happy belief that his affair with Jenny had disrupted Celia's enjoyment of her toy-boy.

Zero hour for the bombshell had not arrived yet, but Celia prepared to walk a perilous tightrope between truth and fiction. Margaret had been involved in the Jenny Watson carry-on, and must know all about the trail of treasure hunt clues leading to Keeper's Cottage. For Celia to pretend to know nothing about that would convict her as a liar. A very economical version of the truth was needed to meet the case.

'Oh, didn't I tell you?' she began. 'That was quite extraordinary, and rather sad. Poor girl, she told me a lot of lies when she applied for the job. Before that she'd worked for a friend of mine who has a small nursery garden in Hampshire, and she'd told lies there too. It turned out that she was creating false identities for herself to hide from two men who were trying to track her down. As you know, they caught up with her in the end and kidnapped her from her lodgings in the village.'

'I wonder why they did that,' pondered Wilfrid Edgeley.

'Because she was an escaped whore, probably,' Grace told him, 'and her whoremaster wanted her back.'

185

'Oh, *no*,' corrected Celia. 'She was kidnapped because she knew too much.'

Margaret failed to keep the eagerness out of her voice. 'What did she know too much about?'

'Ah, that was the fascinating thing,' said Celia, and went on to describe the brilliant feat of detection which had led her to Keeper's Cottage. After giving a blood-curdling description of the sinister exhibits she had found there, she concluded: 'And there were leaflets there about the Green Front that's been in the papers, doing dreadful violent things up and down the country.'

'And that was what the girl knew too much about,' said Fortescue.

'I suppose so. She probably worked for them, then revolted against the idea of violence.'

'So she ran away, but why didn't she tell the police?' Wilfrid demanded.

'She probably promised not to talk,' said Celia, cursing him mentally for asking awkward questions, 'but they didn't trust her not to.'

'You reported all this to the police, I imagine?' asked Margaret.

'Yes. At Amesbury police station.'

'And what did they say?'

'Nothing much, I only saw a sergeant.'

'And nobody higher up contacted you later, even to say thank you?'

'No. The police don't like people who go in for amateur detection, you know. I've been in the dog house with the local force here ever since that business when they accused Bill Wilkins quite wrongly of murder.'

'You were brilliant over that,' gushed Wilfrid, where-upon Grace sniffed audibly.

'Oh, I don't know,' Celia simpered, and managed to look absurdly pleased with herself. 'But they've never forgiven me for making them look silly.'

'The papers say the Green Front is being handled by the Anti-Terrorist Branch,' Margaret prompted.

'Yes. They're much too grand to take any notice of poor

little me. They probably don't know that I even exist.'

'What a pity,' said Fortescue. 'You have this talent for detection. It shouldn't be wasted.'

Taking this flattery at its face value, Celia beamed with fatuous pleasure.

'Don't you ever take up cases for people when the police are going wrong?' Margaret asked.

'No, but I do keep my eyes and ears open when I see something odd.' She took a deep breath and prepared to launch the bombshell. 'Like the other day, for instance. I noticed that a woman I was talking to wasn't a woman at all, but a man dressed up.'

An attentive silence fell.

'When was this?' asked Margaret.

'A few weeks back. My neighbours the Tidmarshes went away and they had to get someone in to look after their livestock. He was calling himself Annabel Johnson, but he was a man.'

'Are you sure?' asked Fortescue very quietly.

'Quite sure, I even know his real name, he's called John Horton and he lives in Wimbledon.'

Margaret choked over her fruit salad and started coughing. Fortescue's charisma vanished. The boot-button eyes glared, as they had done in the confrontation with Admiral Bond. 'How on earth did you find that out?' he asked, managing a grimace of a smile.

'Ah. You see, the Tidmarshes leave their spare key with me, and after Horton had gone I nipped in before they got back, to see what I could see. And – well, one should never neglect waste-paper baskets.'

'You found something?' Margaret asked, only half recovered from her fit of coughing.

Celia nodded mysteriously. 'An envelope, addressed to Annabel Johnson. And there was another envelope inside it, with his name and address on. It had been forwarded from Wimbledon.'

'And you told the police?' asked Fortescue.

'No, why should I? He can be kinky if he likes, it isn't a criminal offence.'

'How about the Tidmarshes? Did you tell them?'

'Of course not. I wouldn't like them to think I'd been nosy and poked around in their house. Don't you tell anyone, will you? I shouldn't really have told you.'

The Fortescues exchanged glances which meant 'careful, that's enough about it for the moment'. They let the subject drop and promoted a move back to the sitting room for coffee. Coming to the rescue of a somewhat laboured conversation, Celia fought down her fears about what would happen next by becoming the slightly hysterical life and soul of the party, prattling about her dislike of the New Guinea *Impatiens*, and of a loathsome bicolour geranium called Aztec, which she had nicknamed 'Montezuma's revenge'. Fortescue gulped down his coffee, rose and excused himself. 'I have some phone calls to make, but don't go, anyone. Margaret, see if they'd like some brandy or a liqueur.'

Margaret obeyed, but no one accepted and she soon began to engineer the little silences which a hostess allows to occur when she has decided that it is time for her guests to go. It was almost indecently early for the party to break up, but Wilfrid took the hint and became uneasy. Asked angrily by his wife why he was fidgeting, he subsided and another half-hour of laborious conversation passed before she thought it polite to make a move. As the Edgeleys left, Margaret seized Celia's arm in a vice-like grip and said: 'Don't go yet. Let's have a cosy girls' gossip.'

'I'm sorry, I really ought to get back.'

'No, really. I'll get them to make us some more coffee.' Before Celia could stop her she hurried out of the room.

Did they really intend to detain her, and if so with what in mind? Fingering the panic button nervously, she went after Margaret, fearing at every turn that Fortescue would leap out at her. But there was no sign of him. Where was he?

Ahead of her, Margaret seemed to be hunting for him. Celia caught up with her. 'Look, I really must go.'

'No, don't.'

It was not quite a command, but too peremptory to be a polite request.

'I must, really.'

Margaret seemed to be wondering what to do. As if hoping to have this decided for her, she shouted: 'Jason! Celia says she must go.' When there was no reply she muttered angrily, 'Where the hell is he?'

There was a long pause. Margaret was a foot taller than Celia and more powerfully built. She made a sudden convulsive movement, then thought better of it and stood there undecided, wondering whether or not her husband wanted Celia detained by force. The fiction that a hostess was pressing a guest to stay longer could still be maintained, but only just.

'Don't go for a minute,' she said, and led the way back into the sitting room. 'There's something I want to tell you.'

Celia sat down facing Margaret.

'I told you earlier that Jason was very protective about me,' Margaret began, 'but it wasn't quite true. He's protective about the idea that his wife has been insulted. That makes him furious because his wife is his property, and insulting his property is insulting him.'

'But you tried to persuade him not to persecute George Bond?'

'No. Trying to persuade Jason of anything is a waste of time. I gave up bothering long ago.'

What was the object of this girls' heart-to-heart? Obviously, to fill in time till Jason surfaced from whatever he was doing, and decided how the situation should be handled.

'Doesn't he listen to you at all?' Celia asked.

She shrugged. 'What do you think?'

'It sounds as if your marriage isn't very happy.'

Margaret gave a short, bitter laugh. 'He married me for the money that started him off in business. It stopped being a marriage in any real sense after the children were born.'

189

'He's away a lot of the time isn't he? How about consolations on the side?'

'Well, what do you think?' said Margaret, smiling and looking smug.

Was there a lover? Or was she simply making conversation, to fill the time till Jason's return? Not necessarily, Celia decided, remembering the story going round the village about a man who visited her at night.

'We are a pair, aren't we?' Margaret added. 'Me with my fancy man and you with your Bill Wilkins.'

Feeling that she ought to do her share of time-filling, Celia decided to be dumbfounded about this scandalous slur on her and Bill's morals. She was just warming to this theme when Jason Fortescue came back from his alleged session on the telephone.

Anxious to get a decision out of him Margaret said: 'Jason dear, Celia says she has to go.'

'Oh, what a shame. Can't you stay for a cup of tea?'

'No, I really can't,' said Celia, relieved. 'I swore to myself that I'd get the accounts up to date this weekend.'

As he escorted her to her car, they chatted amicably about the book-keeping problem of firms too small to employ a full-time accountant. She drove away through the park, feeling very pleased with herself. She had been right. Wilberforce with his panic button and his forebodings of danger had been wrong.

Foster and Grigg, glued to their binoculars in the woods overlooking the park, were as relieved as she was that all was well.

John Horton could not have afforded his luxurious house in Wimbledon on his official wage as the company chauffeur, but it was insignificant compared with the lavish subsidy that he received from one of Fortescue's private accounts. He was relaxing beside his swimming pool after a heavy Sunday lunch when the telephone rang.

'Johnny, it's me, and I'm not pleased. What the hell d'you mean by leaving incriminating documents in waste-paper baskets?'

'I never.'

190

'Oh yes you bloody did. You wait, I'll cut your balls off, you careless bastard.'

'No, chief. Honest. Who says so? Someone's trying to do the dirty on me.'

'Shut up and listen. The Grant woman found an envelope with your real name and address on it in the Tidmarshes' waste-paper basket.'

'No, chief. She couldn't have. I double-checked the whole damn place before I left. She's lying.'

'Then how the hell does she know that your name's John Horton and you live in Wimbledon?'

'Sorry, chief. I don't get that. Come again?'

'She came out with it just now, over lunch. Wasn't it funny, she said. The woman who stood in for the Tidmarshes while they were away was a man in drag. His name's John Horton and he lives in Wimbledon. Just a titbit of local gossip that might interest us, to show what a wide-awake Miss Marple she is.'

'This is crazy, chief. How could the silly bitch have found out?'

'Because you were careless. How dare you leave bits of paper around?'

'Chief, I didn't,' Horton gasped. 'I swear I didn't.'

'You bloody must have. How else could she have got your name?'

Horton thought desperately. 'From the police?'

'How would they know? And why would they want to tell her?'

'She could be working for them.'

'Listen, you clot. She's a half-mad village lady with her nose in her flowerpots and her gardener's prick permanently between her legs. Everyone says she's bone stupid. What would the police want with her? And if the police did find out your name, and she did get it from them, why would she come out with it like that over lunch?'

'Look, chief,' stammered Horton in agony. 'You know me, when have you found me leaving incriminating evidence around? Never. I swear I never left a thing at the Tidmarshes'.'

Fortescue ignored this. 'Balls, Johnny. What you need

191

is a red-hot poker up your arse, to teach you not to be careless. 'Bye now. Stay by the phone, I'll be in touch.'

He believed in keeping key employees in a state of fear. But on thinking it over he admitted to himself that Horton's frantic denials bore the stamp of truth. He had always been a careful worker, to leave an addressed envelope in a waste-paper basket would be most unlike him. There must be some other answer.

He was worried, too, about the fiasco at Frensham and Clark's. He only knew what had been in the papers, but it looked as if Hamilton had fallen into a carefully laid trap. Smithson, their managing director, was a wide-awake operator and quite capable of guessing that the attack would come on a Thursday, when Arkwright would be at the plant. Was it chance that he had set the trap on that particular Thursday? Or was there a traitor some-where around?

All this needed investigating. He made a few arrange-ments to this end, then went back to the sitting room to see Mrs Grant off the premises while the servants were still around to see her go.

He had made one mistake, however. He had unwisely left the wretched Horton in such agony and confusion of mind that he was incapable of coherent thought. In the end Horton remembered the strange behaviour of the police after the burglary at Curzon Street. But by the time he had worked out why they had taken everyone's fingerprints it was too late to ring Kenlake with a warning. Wilberforce's men had acted promptly, and he was shar-ing a cell with two drug addicts at Wimbledon police station.

The phone call had of course been recorded for police purposes, and would be produced in court as evidence of the connection between Fortescue, Horton, and the Green Front. Wilberforce was delighted by the success of the operation at Kenlake, and very relieved that Mrs Grant had come to no harm. He looked forward to con-gratulating her warmly when they met, as arranged, in the car park of a quiet country pub seven miles from Kenlake.

Anxious to protect her from any unpleasantness that Fortescue might contemplate, he had insisted on her leaving Melbury at once on a short holiday. A police escort was to see her safely to the house of friends living near Lewes, where she was to remain till Fortescue was safely locked away behind bars.

But where was she? She was supposed to drive straight to the pub when she left Kenlake, but over an hour had passed.

'She couldn't still be at Kenlake?' Wilberforce asked Grigg. 'You're sure it was her in the car?'

'Yes, chief. Fortescue came out into the drive to shake hands with her, and she drove away.'

Panic set in, followed by a county-wide search. Hours later her car was found in a lay-by near Godalming, with her suitcase still in the boot.

Eleven

The lay-by was on a lonely stretch of road. Mrs Grant had probably been transferred there to another vehicle. Wilberforce's men tried hard to find a witness who had seen it happen, but in vain. According to forensics, her fingerprints on the steering wheel had been overlaid by a driver wearing gloves: a man, to judge from the size.

'Fortescue's got her stashed away somewhere,' said Wilberforce between set teeth. 'He's had second thoughts about that envelope in the waste-paper basket, and he's going to batter the real story out of her.'

'Pull him in and charge him?' Grigg suggested.

'No. If we do that, whoever's holding her for him will kill her, so she can't give evidence against him. No, we watch Kenlake again, see where he goes to interrogate her and follow him.'

Back in their observation post in the woods, Grigg and Foster waited anxiously for Fortescue to lead them to Mrs Grant's hiding place. Nothing of the kind happened. Instead, he installed himself in a deckchair on the lawn with the newspapers, and was presently joined by his wife with a trayful of tea. 'Waiting till it gets dark?' Foster suggested hopefully. But there seemed to be no reason why he should.

Shortly after six, a small car came up the drive and disappeared into the stable yard. 'The staff, coming back from their Sunday afternoon off,' Grigg decided.

'So he's had the place to himself for hours,' said Foster, 'except for his wife and his bully-boys.'

But the relevance of this was not clear to him.

Having finished their tea, the Fortescues went back into the house, and for another hour nothing more happened. Then a small van entered the park. But instead of driving round to the servants' entrance in the stable yard, it parked by the front door.

'Who is it? Can you see?' said Grigg, peering through his glasses.

'A woman. Grey hair. Or – no, I think it's a blonde. Funny, driving up to the posh front door in that grotty little van.'

Marion Underhill had decided that it would be unwise to arrive in the Melbury area in Michael's BMW, so she had borrowed the van from one of his yobbos. She parked it close under the windows of the house and rang the bell.

The gorilla-like manservant who opened the door said he would enquire if Mr Fortescue was at home, and asked her her business. When she said she had a message for him from Michael Hamilton, the man did a startled double-take and let her into the hall.

Presently Jason Fortescue appeared with a table napkin in his hand, chewing. 'You say you have a message for me?' he growled, very much on his guard.

'That's right. From Michael Hamilton.'

Before he could deny knowing any such person she hurried on. 'I'm Michael's girlfriend. I've come to tell you that I'm ready and willing to carry on his work for the environment.'

For a moment the glare of Fortescue's boot-button eyes hid indecision. Then his look softened into a genial smile of welcome. 'Well done, my dear. I'm very glad you came. We must have a long talk, but first, have you eaten? No? Come in then and meet my wife, we were just starting dinner.'

As he ushered her into the dining room she was well pleased with the way things were going. Her research had been thorough. She knew now that Fortescue, far from being a rich and eccentric defender of the environment, owned several companies which were among its worst polluters; that the attack on Frensham and Clark had

195

been in pursuit of a personal vendetta: and that his 'own goal' at his pentachlorophenol plant had been a shrewd business move to get rid of an asset which threatened to become obsolete.

With any luck she would be asked to spend the night. That suited her fine: she would be able to discover the layout of the house, and in particular where Fortescue slept. Despite everything, she was still fighting for the environment, and she was determined to kill him.

The Filipino manservant put a plateful of food in front of her, and the Fortescues began to chat her up. Where had she come from? Liverpool? How depressing, with all that unemployment. Had there been a lot of traffic on the motorway? And *had she told anyone she intended to come to Kenlake*?

'Certainly not. Security's paramount in movements like this, I've a lot of experience.'

The Fortescues exchanged glances. This tiresome girl represented a hair-raising danger, she must be dealt with.

Another problem needed attending to, a very similar one. Thinking about it, Fortescue was not sorry that they had presented themselves on the same evening. In a way it made things easier.

Outside, it was getting dark and Wilberforce was re-organizing. The watchers closed in, covering every way out of Kenlake in case Fortescue slipped away under cover of night to question Mrs Grant. There was still no question of arresting him. He had a hostage, hidden away somewhere and guarded by his bully-boys. Two police-men had seen Mrs Grant leave Kenlake unharmed. Others might have seen her too. There would be no proof that he had been holding her, provided she did not survive to tell the tale. The tap on his telephone had yielded nothing. The only hope was to wait till he made a move.

Celia's head ached and she felt very drowsy. Drifting in and out of consciousness, she realized by degrees that she was tied hand and foot to a chair.

Gradually it all came back to her. Driving out of the park, she had rounded a corner in the avenue of rhododendrons inside the gate when she found the way blocked in front of her by a farm tractor parked crossways on the drive. Before she could reach the panic button, two of Fortescue's bully-boys had dragged her from the car. Where had they taken her? She shut her eyes again, too weary to bother.

She remembered now. They had hauled her, struggling weakly, through the rhododendron belt and into a building on the far side, a shed of some kind that smelt of sheep dip. Then came the prick of a hypodermic, and that was all she could remember.

Where was she now? In an attic, obviously. The walls sloped. Night sky showed through the dormer window, hours must have passed. Where was this attic? Probably at Kenlake.

There was a smell of tobacco. She opened her eyes again and turned her head. In the corner of the room behind her, Margaret Fortescue was reading the *Mail on Sunday* and smoking a cigarette.

'Oh, you're awake, are you?' she said. 'Wait here a moment, I'll be back.' In the doorway she paused, and held up the cigarette. 'If you try shouting while I'm out, I shall burn you with this when I come back.'

She went, leaving Celia to her thoughts, which were disagreeable. When she came back Fortescue was with her. He was carrying a small electrical appliance, which he plugged into the wall.

'Now, Mrs Grant. You know what this is?'

'It looks to me like a soldering iron.'

'That's right, and when it gets hot I shall use it to make you tell me just how you found out John Horton's name and address.'

'Oh, really, this isn't the Middle Ages. Do put that ridiculous thing away, because I have absolutely no objection to telling you. In fact I propose to tell you the whole story of your shocking misbehaviour, starting with the microphones the police found in my office and Admiral

197

Bond's house, and ending with the trap the police laid for your Mr Hamilton at Frensham and Clark's. And when I have finished, you will probably conclude that as the police are likely to arrest you within hours, you will only make matters worse for yourself if you fail to release me unharmed.'

'I don't believe a word of this,' shouted Margaret angrily.

Fortescue quelled her with a look. 'Go on, Mrs Grant. Let's have the detail. All of it.'

Her recital, punctuated by keen questioning from Fortescue, lasted a long time. When it was over, Margaret looked at her reproachfully. 'Oh dear, you're not stupid at all, are you? You're clever and very dangerous. Grace Edgeley got you quite wrong. I could murder her.'

'And I could murder you for not checking out what that silly bitch said,' Fortescue told her. 'Another thing, if you hadn't gone in for those fancy touches about Mrs Grant's gardener and that blonde nuisance who's snoring in the blue bedroom, we wouldn't be in this mess. All the fault of that lover of yours.'

'Michael Hamilton isn't my lover,' said Margaret in a shocked voice.

'Oh yes he is, I've known about it for over a year.'

Changing her stance, she shrugged. 'Well, what did you expect? You've paid me no attention for ages. He cares. He was furious with Mrs Grant here for letting the Admiral get away with insulting me. We decided it would be fun to punish her by enticing her toy-boy away from her. And it helped your business along at the same time.'

'On the contrary, it wrecked the whole show.'

'Bill is not my toy-boy,' Celia interrupted in a fury.

Fortescue's eyes swivelled round to her. 'God, what are we to do with her?'

'Let her go, of course. What else?'

'No! She'd give evidence against me.'

'There's plenty of that without her.'

'When people play filthy tricks on me, I don't forgive them that easily.'

198

'There you go again! When someone upsets you, you behave like a vicious child.'

'Shut up, damn you. Let me think.'

The tense silence which followed was broken only by little whimpering exclamations from Margaret. Then, suddenly, a sound of scuffling began outside the door. It opened, and one of the bully-boys dragged Marion Underhill into the room. She was fully dressed, and had her few possessions with her in a tote bag.

'She climbed out of a first-floor window,' the bully-boy reported. 'We caught her trying to start her car.'

'Really? I wonder why,' said Fortescue. 'Come in, Marion, and let me introduce you to Michael Hamilton's other girlfriend.'

Marion looked Margaret up and down contemptuously. 'You're no girlfriend of my Michael's. He just makes a habit of giving his bosses' wives a casual fuck or two, however old and ugly they are. He gets a kick out of it, he told me so. It's his way of cocking a snook at the pompous shits who employ him.'

Margaret raged at this, but Fortescue ignored her. 'That's enough of that,' he snapped, and hit Marion hard across the face. 'What I want to know is, what were you doing out by your car when you were supposed to be in bed and asleep?'

'I . . . was restless. I'm used to living rough, all this sick luxury here turned me up. I couldn't sleep.'

This did not satisfy him, and he went on needling her. Her answers became more and more tetchy and distracted, and she kept looking at her watch.

Celia could stay silent no longer. 'Marion's obviously worried about the time. I think she came here to punish you as a polluter of the environment. She wasn't trying to start her car, she was setting the timer of the bomb in it. And now she's worried about when it will go off.'

In the stunned silence which followed, Marion said: 'Damn you, Mrs Grant, why couldn't you keep your mouth shut?'

'Because I have no wish to be blown up while sitting on this very uncomfortable chair.'

Fortescue was smiling strangely. 'Well, well, this is very convenient. You've solved several knotty problems for me all in one. Come on, Benson. Let's go.'

Followed by the bully-boy he strode out of the room and locked the door behind him on the outside.

Margaret flung herself against it, sobbing and shrieking. 'Jason! Let me out, don't be like this. I've always done what you wanted, haven't I? Jason!'

She was answered only by footsteps thundering down the stairs.

As Margaret's lamentations continued, Celia said 'Marion, quick. There's a gadget on a string round my neck, inside my dress. It's a panic button for calling the police. Pull it out and press it. That's right, go on pressing it, hard.'

In Grigg's car, parked in the lane just outside the park, something bleeped. 'What was that?' asked Foster.

As the bleep continued, Grigg looked down. 'Christ! It's Mrs Grant's panic button.' He picked up the phone to call Wilberforce. 'She must have been in there all this time.'

Within seconds, four police cars were speeding up the drive towards the house. But a pair of powerful headlights were heading the opposite way. Fortescue in his Porsche was distancing himself from Marion's bomb.

Only yards ahead of the leading police car, the Porsche swerved off the drive and bounded past all four cars on the springy turf. Detailed by Wilberforce, two of the cars turned to give chase, while the others pressed on towards the house.

'This damn place is big enough to house the homeless of London,' Marion grumbled as she untied Celia. 'Even if the fuzz heard your gadget go off, they'd never find us up here in the time.'

'How about the window?' said Celia, massaging her ankles. 'Let's look.'

It was stuck shut, but Marion smashed it open with a chair. As usual with Georgian houses, the wide gutter running round the roof outside was hidden behind an ornamental parapet.

200

'Would we be better off out there?' Celia wondered.

'Only if there's a fire escape.'

Margaret was still sobbing hysterically by the door. Celia seized her by the shoulders and shook her. 'Is there one? Is there a fire escape we could get down?'

Choking back sobs, Margaret nodded.

Marion pushed her towards the window. 'Come on then, Deirdre of the Sorrows, show us where it is.'

Wilberforce had to ring and batter on the front door for over five minutes before a frightened Filipino opened it. He knew only that Mrs Grant had left after lunch, and was surprised at the suggestion that she might be back in the house. The other servants were equally ignorant, and Fortescue's bully-boys had made themselves scarce. A hurried search of the rooms on the ground and first floors produced no result. Wilberforce and Padstow had started on the sparsely furnished second-floor bedrooms when Grigg called to him up the stairs. 'Chief. There's someone shouting, out in the stable yard.'

Wilberforce flung up a window. Far below, he saw a small figure standing in the moonlight. 'Oh, it's you, Mrs Grant. Thank goodness.'

'Listen, there's a bomb somewhere here, in a car. Get everyone out at once, as far from the house as possible.'

Celia, Margaret, the servants, and the police were soon streaming away across the park. They were only just in time. Behind them a huge explosion set off a shock wave which blasted them all forward on to their faces on the grass. A blinding flash lit up the gracious classical front of Kenlake Manor. Then suddenly its stonework disintegrated, hanging in the air for a moment like the drops of a waterfall photographed in slow motion. Then the waterfall crashed down. A cloud of smoke rose from it, and as it cleared, fires started in the shattered rooms behind the façade.

'Why did Fortescue want to let off a bomb?' Wilberforce wondered, picking himself up.

'Oh, it wasn't his,' said Celia. 'Marion Underhill brought it here, to kill him with.'

'Really? I wonder why?' He looked round. 'Where is she?'

201

Celia pointed towards the little van, which was burning fiercely. 'She went to try and defuse the bomb. Poor girl. She was very brave.'

'But very wrong-headed,' said Wilberforce severely.

Meanwhile two squad cars were chasing Fortescue through the country lanes at over a hundred miles an hour. He was taking hair-raising risks, it was only a matter of time before he came to grief. Presently he lost control at a sharp bend and smashed the Porsche against a tree.

He was still conscious when they put him in the ambulance. Ingrained habit took over, and he began hazily sketching out a version of events at Kenlake which left him blameless. 'Such a tragedy . . . my poor dear wife. Why wasn't I more careful, I should have known that those Green Front people would try to get me . . .'

He died two hours later in hospital.